SOLE

A NOVEL

Elspeth Grafton

Dearest Pat!
I hope you enjoy reading this
as much as I enjoyed writing
it!
          Much love,
               Elspeth 2013

elspethgrafton@gmail.com

Sole is privately published, and printed by Black Crow Books. Information about Black Crow Books can be found at:

blackcrowbooks.com

ISBN 978-0-9918595-0-4
Ebook ISBN 978-0-9918595-1-1

Copy layout and design: Brian Grafton

Cover image: Gary Friedman/www.FriedmanArchives.com
Cover design: Brian Grafton

SOLE

Hopes, wants and desires comprise our dreams.
But the sole need is self-awareness.

From the unwritten *ABCs of Life*

To the Reader

WELCOME TO the world of *Sole*.

Sole is the baby of my first *NaNoWriMo* (National Novel Writing Month), an online challenge where aspiring writers are given the thirty days of November to write a 50,000 word novel. That's 1600 words a day. For most people, writing 1600 words per day, every day, is daunting. It was daunting for me too, but I did it!

Approaches to the *NaNoWriMo* challenge vary. Some people spend the months leading up to November planning, plotting, and formulating their characters. Others envision entire worlds and technologies before they begin. I chose a different path. I had one solitary image in my head and decided, as my writing guru Julia Cameron suggests in her book *The Right to Write*, to have faith, pick up my pen and WRITE.

As a result, my creative life changed.

One image turned into the first chapter, then the second. And so on. No planning, no plotting, just faith that there was story to tell, that my characters would keep talking to me, and that I could accurately write down the movie that was playing in my head.

What you're about to read has had no professional editing. What you're about to read has had one rewrite, which also added the epilogue. What you're about to read is pretty much as it was originally written. From sentence one, day one.

In seeing *Sole* to print, I have so many people to thank. I have my creative soul sisters, Nicole Myers and Kiersten Johnston, without whom I would never have had the courage not only to put pen to paper, but actually to allow people to read my creations.

I have my fantastic family who, when they heard I was doing *NaNoWriMo* said, "You're doing what?", and then supported every word, reading first drafts and loving (or hating) it. They were honest with their feedback and that was invaluable. It still is, and you all know who you are!

My wonderful Mum and Da (yes, Da: not a typo) get a special thank you. My Mum's unwavering support and encouragement held me up on the days when I thought it was all crap and I didn't want to write another word. She's an avid reader, and having her spend her spare precious time and skill on first drafts was like offering a part of my being and having it cherished and returned wrapped in a bow. Getting my father's nod of approval on any writing project means the world. Getting this story printed is his gift to me.

I adore them both more than mere words can say and am thankful every day that the combination of traits these two possess resulted in my desire to write.

Of course, the last thank you is to you – the reader. Thank you for choosing to spend your precious time reading this little tale. I can only hope you have as much fun reading this as I did writing it, and that the movie that was playing in my head as I wrote it comes alive in your imagination as you read.

Elspeth Grafton
Vancouver, BC
2013

ONE

LUCINDA MACHAULEY was a bitch, self-proclaimed and unashamed. Her parents knew it; her lover knew it; and any of her coworkers who'd had a run-in with her steered clear of her because of it. Her behavior, tone of voice, and her basic overall demeanor was tolerated due to the fact that Lucinda had three older brothers, some exceptional talents in the bedroom, and was exceedingly good at her job.

Everything Lucinda did had a purpose. No movement was wasted; even the tailoring she had done on all her clothing was efficient. She was small of stature and slim; both belied her strength and the ferocity with which she could cut someone down with a stare. If she thought it necessary to talk with you, you were certainly going to leave the conversation knowing who'd been holding the talking stick most of the time, and you'd probably feel a couple of pounds lighter as she'd have torn a strip or two off of you just for kicks. And that same control, that overwhelming need to assert power, was exactly what had initially attracted and had kept Hank Willis tied to Lucinda's side – or tied to her bed, depending on the evening. He was enthralled by her, and she in turn was surprised that a man like Hank had been willing to give up the reins in their relationship for an extended length of time.

Lucinda was spending a restless night at home. It was Saturday night, and after glancing briefly at her watch for the umpteenth time in the span of an hour, she realized, with a resigned sigh, that Hank had stood her up. Again. This was the second Saturday in a row, and she was far from impressed. She sighed heavily, rubbing her long fingers through her jet-black pixie hair cut. Just as things were looking so promising, she thought to herself. Ah well, onto bigger, better, and more trainable... She reached into the purse that was sitting on her kitchen counter and extracted the compact cell phone tucked inside. She held the phone between her two hands, and with precise movements of her thumbs, she deleted all phone numbers for Hank Willis. She dropped the cell back into its appropriate spot in her purse, and strode determinedly into her bathroom. The second toothbrush that sat in the ceramic coffee mug next to her sink was immediately tossed in the garbage, as was the Mennen deodorant that Lucinda found in the cabinet below. Her steps were firm as she headed into her bedroom and brushed the gossamer fabric that concealed her closet to one side. There was little evidence on the shelves on the right hand side of the closet that Hank had been part of her world for the last six months. One tattered t-shirt, and a pair of blue boxer shorts. Both were quickly removed and unceremoniously trashed.

Having cleansed her apartment of these unwanted items, Lucinda couldn't think what to do with herself. She felt uncharacteristically...what...what was this feeling... loneliness? At this realization, Lucinda huffed out of her bedroom toward the kitchen. The curses she tossed to the universe hung in the air, clouding her vision, clouding her ability to feel. She grabbed a beer, wrenched the cap from the top and drank deeply, before she realized that the beer was a type that he liked. She ended up dumping the unfinished bottle down the drain. That made her feel slightly satisfied, and slightly better.

Lucinda wandered slowly back into her bedroom. She could still go out tonight. There was still time. It was New York City after all. Things were barely getting started at this time of night. She took a quick glance into her open closet, surveying the many outfits, as yet unworn, that waited to strike her fancy. Her sight rested on one wire coat hanger, shoved to the far

far left hand side, tucked behind the first designer suit she'd been able to afford, an article she couldn't bear to throw away despite it being tragically out of fashion. She smiled lightly to herself. No. Tonight she'd take care of herself.

She reached for the garment on the wire hanger and pulled it loose, leaving the hanger swinging empty on the clothing rod. She rolled the thin, familiar fabric through her fingers before tossing it on the bed. Yes, she decided, tonight she was going to do a little work from home. Although the Lucinda MacHauley of Manolo Blahnik's Madison Avenue office wouldn't be welcomed anywhere near where she was thinking of venturing tonight, I.S.Y.S (I'll Sell Your Sole) would be, both at the Leather.com site and at Anne Cole's website.

Manolo had been doing booming business since the 'Sex and the City' franchise had unashamedly been plugging its wares. Thank you Candice Bushnell, Lucinda thought as she unzipped the low heeled leather boots that clung tightly to her calves and tossed them into the bottom of the closet. She unbuttoned the crisp white blouse and meticulously hung it next to four others in her closet. Her skirt, being gun-metal gray tweed, was easy to care for and was returned to its solo hanger. Delicates tossed in the laundry pile, Lucinda reached over to where the old nightgown lay on her duvet. She paused only momentarily before she allowed herself to put it on.

As the caress of faded flannel draped her, part of her felt the pressure of city life – the pressure she put on herself, the pressure for perfection – slide down and off her body. Part of her became 'just plain ole' Lucy from Monona Iowa'. But only part of her: she still had a job to do tonight. Lucinda hummed to herself as she booted up her laptop and sat in front of it on her bed with legs crossed. Market research could never stop. There were always new markets to reach, new consumers to enlighten. It was her job to make sure they got the message. And if they were smart, they did, and fast.

TWO

OLIVER GARCIA shed his business persona as he pulled the loosened necktie over his head and meticulously hung it beside countless others in his closet. He casually unbuttoned his Dolce & Gabana dress shirt and pulled it free of his trousers as he walked the five paces to his dresser. Leaving his shirt gaped open, he reached deeply into his pockets. One fist revealed a sparse ring (one car key, office and apartment key, and one security fob) which he placed delicately on the polished surface of his dresser. The other fist contained several slightly creased business cards, which he plucked from amongst loose change and placed neatly in a pile next to the key ring.

The remaining change was drizzled into a small, wide wicker basket. Oliver smiled softly to himself. Ah, the sound of money. He picked the business cards back up and tried to flatten them back into perfection. Despite the effort he wasn't successful, so he tucked them into the wallet that had been neatly stowed in his back pocket. Out of sight out of mind? Not likely, but it was the best he could do. The wallet was quickly deposited on top of the change.

As a young boy, Oliver had watched his father follow this same post-work routine – except that his father had first pulled off contractor-type overalls, not a Brooks Brothers tie, and the pants that had held his little bit of spare change had been well-worn dungarees, not Armani twill. If young Oliver had done his parents proud by bringing home an exceptionally fine report card, or had scored in a local soccer league game, he would be rewarded by being allowed to count the change in the wide ceramic saucer. Occasionally Oliver's father would sit next to him, and help him to keep the stacks of coins

5

straight. But more often than not, Oliver was left to his own devices, a pool of coins spread before him on the faded floral quilt that covered his parents' double bed.

Oliver ran his fingertips over the coins that sat in his own wicker basket visible under the soft leather wallet, then he caressed the rim, relishing in the difference between smooth coin and rough reed. He sighed at the memory, gave his head a quick shake, then returned to his closet.

His pants hung up and his soiled shirt placed in the dry cleaning bag, Oliver lazily made his way across the room, making a mental note to drop the items off on his way to the office on Monday. He casually flipped the power on the Bang & Olufsen stereo system, allowing the first strains of piano from "ABBA's Greatest Hits" to come blaring out of the speakers. Oliver stripped off his boxer briefs, tossed them to the floor of the closet, shut the doors against the mess, and padded barefoot into his tiled bathroom. He cranked the shower's hot water tap open as far as was possible, and as the hiss of water struck the marble tiling, Oliver turned and inspected his face in the mirror.

There was no questioning his heritage. Slightly olive skin, the type that tans so easily, dark chocolate eyes, surrounded by fine laugh lines, looked back at him. Those lines, he thought to himself, those lines are the only things that betray my true age. The last lover he'd taken had thought he was 25, the one before had believed he was 27. Oliver laughed lightly to himself, straightened up, and rubbed his hands down his chest and over his flat abs. Yes, he thought, I can still get away with it – barely.

He leaned back closer to the mirror and poked at the laugh lines once again, and recalled his father whose leathery, constantly tanned face was a result of many, many years working on construction sites, or on highway crews. Oliver made another mental note for Monday: call Julio to get the name of his plastic surgeon. Those lines had to go. With that thought, Oliver stepped under the blistering spray of his shower, and allowed the steam to carry the weight of his day off his shoulders.

∞

Emerging cleansed, buffed, and as exfoliated as was humanly possible without heading down to the spa, Oliver felt rejuvenated as he casually wrapped a plush cotton towel around his waist. He inspected the five o'clock shadow that appeared on his cheeks and chin, debating whether to shave. Without sparing another thought, Oliver reached deep into the cabinet beneath the sink and removed a plain, battered cardboard box, placing it without ceremony beside his shaving kit on the counter. He carefully inspected the thick tape that sealed the lid. Everything was still in place – "Batteries/ Electric Razor" was scrawled boldly in black Sharpie across the lid.

Oliver casually flipped the box onto its top, and with practiced ease, slid the bottom flaps from where they were knotted together. He sighed deeply, contentedly as he removed the towel from the top, and scanned the contents. From the dark corners of the box, Oliver pulled out a bottle of moisturizer, and inspected the label, 'Lavender Butter' by L'Occitane. His favorite, he thought, as he unscrewed the cap and inhaled the scent deeply. He liberally applied the cream to his face and neck, feeling his demeanor change with each pass of his hand over his skin. Yes, Oliver thought, starting to sing out loud with the music, tonight is going to be a fabulous night.

He was caught off guard by a ringing phone. He ducked his head out of the bathroom doorway, his eyes darting to his iPhone. The screen remained dark. It wasn't his cell phone interrupting him; it was his landline. He hastily glanced at his watch as he crossed to the night stand. Oliver knew that this couldn't be one of the friends or acquaintances that he was meeting with. They only had his mobile number. He picked up the hand set with slight trepidation.

"Hello?"

"Oliver, thank goodness you're home." The familiar, gravelly voice seemed to crackle over the line.

"Of course Mama, where else would I be? I've been at work all day – on a Saturday too. I'm bone tired."

"Ah," his mother sighed, "Oliver, you're doing your father's memory – God rest his soul! – proud with all your hard work. You're all I could ask for a son."

Oliver could see, in his mind's eye, his mother, kerchief in one hand, hair in curlers, and an old dressing gown on, crossing herself as she sat at the same laminate kitchen table where he had eaten all his meals and done his lessons when he was growing up.

"What's going on, Mama? Are you okay? You're sounding tired."

She sighed into the mouthpiece of the phone, as if there were a need to emphasize what he said. "Oh Ollie. I'm so tired. I don't seem to sleep anymore. Since your father, God rest his soul, left me here... ." She sniffled loudly, and Oliver, used to this routine, sat heavily on the side of his bed. "Oliver, what would I do without you? You running his business – well, I suppose it's your business now – you won't forget about your old Mama here in this house all alone, will you?"

These dramatics didn't sway Oliver in the least. He was used to this – he got a call like this from his mother at least once a week. He knew he'd just have to talk her through it. "Mama, you're hardly alone. Where is Rosella Maria? She got a date tonight?"

"Pffft." Oliver visualized his mother shaking her kerchief as she talked. "That girl. I have no control over her. She is seventeen going on forty. She's more than I can handle. Will you talk with her, Olly? When you come over next? Come over for supper tomorrow night, or come over for breakfast tomorrow – I'll make your favorite. We can head out to church afterwards. You are still taking me to church aren't you?"

"Mama, there hasn't been a Sunday in the last five years that I haven't accompanied you to church. Of course I'll be there in the morning. But breakfast? I don't know. I was hoping to have a bit of a lie-in as I was at work early this morning." More like he was hoping to have a bit of extra time to sleep off his hangover. He had been looking forward to heading out on the town.

"Oliver, you never come over anymore. You're Mr. Big-Shot now, I guess, living in the city on your own. How are you ever going to give me a grandbaby if you are always working, and you never come back to the neighborhood, so you aren't meeting any of the nice young ladies here? You know, Conchetta Rodriguez? Do you remember her? She lives with her mother at the end of the block. Well, she's single again. Should I invite her over for dinner tomorrow night? You haven't seen her since high school. Dios Mio, you would make beautiful babies together..."

Oliver sighed to himself, and tuned his mother out. Now that she had started on this tangent, it would be difficult to get her off the phone. This was a constant battle with his mother. Being the elder child, and the only male, he was *expected* to procreate prolifically within the holy strictures of Mother Church and thus continue the Garcia line. He knew it worried his mother that he was 35 and unattached. But she would hardly approve of his potential mate. Oliver allowed his sight to rest on the edge of the cardboard box sitting on his bathroom counter. It was just visible past the doorjamb. He inhaled deeply and focused again on his mother's rant.

"Without your father here, you've stepped in like a true professional, Oliver. Your Papa would be so very proud of you. We've seen increased production while you've been at the helm, and we've bid on three projects in the last two weeks alone. All right, Ollie, you *have* been working hard. You deserve to sleep late tomorrow morning. Don't worry about coming around for breakfast. You need your sleep. But you'll pick me up before church?"

"Of course, Mama. I'll be at your doorstep by nine tomorrow. And try to get some sleep tonight, Mama. You worry too much. I'm taking care of everything. You haven't a care in the world. And I'll call Rosella Maria on Monday and see if we can talk. I'll find out what's going on with her. I doubt she'll be up early enough to talk with me tomorrow morning."

"You're such a good boy, Oliver. I knew you wouldn't forget about us here."

"Of course I won't forget. I love you, Mama. I love Rosella Maria too. You are my family. Family first, isn't that what Papa used to say?" Oliver cursed himself as soon as he'd uttered the words. Why couldn't he just keep his gob shut!

True to form, this last comment started a new blaze of tears from his mother, and pretty much put a kibosh on his plans for the evening. After all this talk of family, faith and father – at times, Oliver saw them as the worst three f-words in any lexicon – there was no way he was heading out to "The Black Hole" tonight. His friends would be disappointed. This would be the second weekend in a row he'd bailed on them with no notice. Ah well, they'd just have to deal.

"Mama?" He interrupted later, knowing that to save his sanity he had to get off the phone, "Mama," he said again, talking right over her, "Mama I have to go. My cell phone is ringing ... the music? In the background? It's ABBA, Mama. You know ABBA. The group. I took you to go see 'Mama Mia' last month ... yes ... that's the one ... I'm glad you had fun, Mama. Yes, I'll see you in the morning ... I love you too, Mama .... Good night." Oliver had practically hung up while his mother was still talking. He felt guilty, and his spirit was deflated. But hearing his mother talk about his father usually did that to him.

He glanced at the watch that banded loosely to his wrist, and then the thin leather band knotted beside it. It was already after ten. He no longer felt like going out to drink and dance. He no longer felt like he was able to go out and hook up with anyone. Oliver now felt weighted and old. Thanks Mama, he thought to himself as he shuffled back into his bathroom. He rubbed a hand over his suddenly weary face. A waft of lavender struck him. Okay, the thought, he wouldn't go out tonight. He would indulge himself at home instead.

Standing in front of his tried and true cardboard box, Oliver reached inside and picked up the first vial that his fingers touched. He removed the lid gingerly and rolled up the contents. Not quite right. He popped the vial back in the box.

A second, third and fourth vial suffered the same treatment, until he found one that struck his fancy. There was usually a routine that accompanied this search. There was usually a a ritual of sorts that was adhered to when heading out for the evening. Routine kept him together. But not tonight. Tonight, Oliver was staying in. He rolled the next tube between his fingers, and rolled the contents up the shaft. 'Morning Song Mauve' suited his mood of this evening; 'Morning Song Mauve' would be this evening's companion.

He pursed his lips and slowly, delicately and deliberately, he ran the waxy color over his own lips. Yes. This was perfect. His hands shook slightly as he traced the bow of his lips, causing the color to betray the natural line. He cursed lightly under his breath and reached back into the box for some remover. Once he had erased his mistake, he tried again, and this time was successful. He ran his lips over each other, slowly, sensuously, and then leaned back to inspect the result. Perfect. Beautiful.

That task accomplished, Oliver hung up the towel that had remained around his waist since his shower, and headed back into his bedroom. He re-opened his closet doors and slipped on the dark burgundy silk robe that hung there. He tied the sash tightly around his slim hips, and stood on tiptoes to reach a suitcase resting in the far back corner of the upper shelf. The case slid easily from where it had been hidden, and Oliver brought it down and rested it in front of the shoe horse tucked in the back of the closet. With practiced ease, he opened each catch and flipped the lid fully open. His breath caught as it did each time he allowed himself to indulge in the contents of this case. He used the same discerning eye he had in choosing his lip color for the evening. Packages were lifted, inspected and set aside until the perfect pair was in his hand. Basic black was his choice, with a light weave fishnet. Excellent. He closed the lid of the case but didn't return it to the shelf.

He gingerly opened the plastic wrapping on the stockings, and carefully shook the hose free, allowing his fingers to whisper over the tight weave of the netting. He sighed with contentment. He draped the hose over one silk sleeve, and walked into the office that adjoined his bedroom. He didn't bother to turn on the overhead light or the desk lamp next to the keyboard, opting to turn on his computer and finish his preparations by the glow if his monitor. As his hard drive was booting up, Oliver propped each foot in turn on his office chair and slid the hose slowly up each calf, over his knee to the muscular thigh. He wriggled his toes, enjoying the feel of the net catching slightly on his toenails.

His 'stay-up hose' firmly in place, Oliver opened the bottom drawer of his desk, and pulled out a shoebox with '2007 Tax Receipts' written boldly across the top. He lifted the lid and revealed his pride and joy. He pulled out one patent black pump, and let his fingers slide over the shiny surface. Sitting, he buffed a slight scuff with one silken sleeve, then placed the shoe on the ground next to his feet. The second shoe received the same inspection, and found its way next to its partner on the buff carpet. Oliver replaced the lid on the box and swiveled to tuck it out of sight. As he slipped his feet into the delicious leather heels only one word ran through his brain. Idyllic, he thought, just idyllic.

He moved aside the sides of his robe and inspected his calves and size 11 feet. I have great legs, he thought to himself. Too bad no one else will see them tonight. With a sigh he got up, and with all the grace his six-foot tall frame would allow, he sashayed into the kitchen, and poured himself a glass of chardonnay. He brought the chilled glass back with him to the office, and found his computer system ready and waiting for him. He took a sip of the crisp wine and hunkered down for an evening on the Internet.

THREE

JULIAN RUFAILO, head bowed, sat with his parents around
their dining room table. He absentmindedly switched between
pushing mushy peas around his plate, and tucking a wisp of
straight light brown hair that had escaped his pony-tail back
behind his ear, letting the argument his parents were having
flow over his head.

They had been bickering for the last twenty five years,
but adored each other, and had raised Julian, their only son,
with a healthy respect for individual opinion. His parents had
taught him to be true to himself, his opinions and beliefs.
He had grown up with political debates over the breakfast
table. Although Julian's parents, Isaak and Margot, were both
Democrats, Isaak tended to lean a little more to the right than
his loving wife, so much discussion and debate had ensued
over the years. As a family, they had been extremely involved,
marching together for various causes, attending symposia
on various issues at MOMA, and indulging in passionate
arguments at all times. Despite the knock down, drag 'em out
debates that happened almost daily, the Rufailo household
allowed differences of opinion to wash away as each day
closed and they hugged and kissed each other good night.

When Julian had come to the realization about his sexual
orientation at the awkward age of 15, he had felt completely
comfortable coming out to his folks. There were a few tears
shed over grandchildren that would never be, but as reality set
in, his parents reacted as they had always done. They researched
the issue; checked their political and personal commitments,
and – though they bickered about the fine points, both joined
a group advocating gay and lesbian rights – "Parents, Families

& Friends of Lesbians and Gays". Ever since, Margot had been integrally involved in PFLAG Chapter 16 (from the Hudson River to the East River and central Park South to 125th Street). She had her hands full. Isaak, on the other hand, although he loved and respected his son dearly, thought that PFLAG was a bit too New Age for his taste. Being gay wasn't a crime, it wasn't a deviation, but why parade it around? With all the discrimination and hate crimes still occurring across the country, he swallowed any misgivings he might have about the means and just decided to support his son, come hell or high water.

Julian was so caught up in his own torment he only caught snippets of the argument that was raging between his parents. PFLAG potato salad. Who the fuck cares about potato salad, Julian thought. My heart is broken, it has been for months, and neither of you have taken the time to see it. Neither of you know. If you could stop arguing for five minutes and take a breather, I'd tell you. His parents were arguing over the PFLAG picnic tomorrow in Central Park, an event his mother had helped organize.

Julian's mind wasn't on the quantity of food being prepared for the event, Julian was concerned about who was actually going to be in the park tomorrow afternoon. Christophe. Christophe, the French-Canadian love of his life, the love of his life who had up and left New York without so much as a kiss on the cheek. Well, it was rumored that he was going to be at the picnic with his new boyfriend. Julian shook his head and roughly pushed his chair back from the table.

The legs squealed harshly against the hardwood floors that were prevalent through out this brownstone, loud enough to pause his parents mid-sentence. They both looked up at him with wide eyes, questioning this odd behavior.

Stammering "I'm, uh, not hungry" as his chair stopped its grating, Julian quickly left the table, heading up the narrow staircase to his room. Once in his sanctuary, Julian tried to drown out the raised voices of his parents that carried up through the floor, their argument continuing despite his departure. No amount of soundproofing could ever drown out their heated words.

His mother was concerned that the potato salad that she'd prepared wasn't going to be enough for the number of people who had RSVP'd for the event. She was trying to persuade her husband to head back down to the market to pick up more potatoes; he was resisting, knowing that if he did go shopping, his wife would then be up half the night in the kitchen, and he and Julian would be obligated to haul bowls and bowls of salad across the park from their town house, and would be required to haul any remnants back afterward. Isaak liked potato salad, but didn't relish eating it as leftovers for the next week. The argument continued back and forth as Margot got up and cleared the dinner plates. Julian knew this as her voice became more faint as she entered the kitchen.

Julian went over to his computer, hit the start button, and slipped his favorite CD into his computer. He grabbed the minute earphones from his iPod, and plugged them into the laptop. As his computer was booting up, he stood to his full height, catching his reflection in the small mirror that he'd placed above his desk. Julian turned his head slightly in each direction, examining, and critiquing the features that were before him. His cheekbones had become more pronounced over the two months, as he'd lost a bit of weight through lack of appetite. It's surprising how a breakup can shrink the size of your stomach. His hair, even though it was pulled off of his face in a ponytail, looked lackluster. This only accentuated the slight hollows under each cheekbone, making his lean cheeks look gaunt. Julian licked one fingertip and drew it across what had once been a very stylish and sculpted eyebrow. He'd let things slip. Too many things had been pushed by the wayside; even his appearance was suffering. The pale green eyes reflecting back at him had looked exceedingly green over the last few days, mainly because they were slightly bloodshot from tears unshed.

He tilted his head back, examining the bottom of his chin, and rubbed a smooth knuckle underneath. He was blessed with little beard growth, which helped in his evening pursuits. Yes, he thought to himself, I should go out tonight. He should go out and be around his friends. They would help him to forget that Christophe was in town. They wouldn't let him wallow, as he would if he stayed in this house.

He looked about him, around his childhood room. Whereas the rest of the house had remained dark with the original heavy wood paneling found in homes at the turn of the century, his room was painted an eggshell white, with deep Grecian blue accents around the doorjambs and window frames. He had replaced the posters of pop boy-bands that had adorned his walls as a teenager with a select few framed photographs. His surroundings now were serene in nature, but captured the contrasting elements of his persona entirely. He could be as flamboyant as the next gay man, but tended to keep that attribute restricted to when he left the house as Julia. Yes, Julian, bless his heart, was a well-known drag queen in New York City. He was best known for his lip-syncing ability, renowned throughout the city for his imitation of Celine Dion. The aquiline nose – a genetic gift from his mother – and his long light brown hair made the transformation quite easy. With an expert hand, some strategic padding and a few hot rollers, he could transform himself into the most strikingly beautiful woman.

He placed a hand on either side of his computer, and bent his head as low as it could go, stretching out the tension that hung around his neck like an albatross. This position allowed his ponytail to drag to the front of his shoulder and flop forwards, so the hairs tickled his jaw line. He allowed the file-o-fax in his brain to pick up speed, flipping through, discarding, or saving the names of Soho clubs that would have performances tonight. He remembered contact names and addresses of these clubs with the ease of anyone else remembering their home address.

It was a 'gift', his parents had told him. It was 'remarkable', his teachers had explained. 'Incredible', the admissions board at NYU had written across his application form when his parents had pushed him to apply at the tender age of 16. To Julian, it was little more than a party trick, and at times could be a royal pain in the ass. He could remember details he wished he could forget. He remembered passages from books he'd read when he was seven years old. Julian figured that it came in handy only when, as he'd just done, he was looking for a place to perform or he was standing on stage and could remember details and lyrics from any tune that was played by the DJ.

Julian sighed. He could remember every pained nuance in his conversations with Christophe. He should have known, seen it coming. Moving to the second closet in his room, he slowly pulled the door open. The hinges squeaked in protest, and Julian once again made a mental note to get the oil can from the back broom closet the next time he was down in the kitchen. He pulled on the lone string that hung down from the bare light bulb in the ceiling. Sequins and shimmering fabric blinked back at him under the glaring light. He allowed one hand to slowly caress its way across the shoulders of all the dresses and blouses that hung on their hangers, relishing in the tactile differences in all of them. Hmmm, he thought to himself. Do I want to vamp it up tonight or go classic?

He closed his eyes, allowing his hand to make another pass across each hanger's shoulder. His fingers paused on one fabric or another, allowing himself to savour the feel of each one, absorbing the emotions or memories each evoked. Slowing his breathing, he passed along again until he found the one that felt just right.

For Julian, drag had never been simply a question of 'dressing up'; it was a question of expanding himself to support Julia's flamboyant persona, leaving his own shyness and social awkwardness behind. Julia wasn't someone different per se: she was just 'Julian+'.

His fingers lightly caressed one garment and he knew by touch, without opening his eyes, which dress he'd be wearing tonight. It was a deep, rich blue silk, with plunging neckline, and long sleeves. Yes, he sighed, this is the one. It had cost him a pretty penny at the time he'd purchased it, and had only been worn on a few, special occasions. Tonight was going to be one of them. In his current state of depression, he owed it to Julia to look like a million bucks. He lifted the hanger from the rod and pulled the dress free, then slowly opened his eyes.

Contentedly, he hung the dress on the door of the closet and knelt down to inspect his shoes. He knew the pair that should accompany the dress; it was just a case of finding them in the mountain of heels, boots, loafers, and pumps that were strewn across the floor of his closet. He found one easily, but the second was elusive. He dug deeper, cursing his depressive state. How had he let things get so bad? His closets were never so disorganized! Finally, he found the vagrant pump pressed up against the back wall. He laid both below the dress and stood, feeling his knees crack lightly.

Having determined that 'Glamorous' Celine would be making an appearance tonight, the rest of his preparations came to mind in easy order. Julian felt his spirit lift. He'd made the right decision. Going out tonight was exactly what he needed to do. Tomorrow would be whatever it was meant to be. Christophe would show or he would not. He'd have his boy-toy with him or he would not. Julian recognized that he didn't have much control over it. Tonight, however, he could take the reins and be exactly who he wanted to be. He could be with whomever he chose (and in the past he'd been much in demand at the clubs). With renewed purpose, he left his room, and entered the pristine bathroom that was next door.

The cabinet that was underneath his sink was very distinctly dual. The left side, with the innumerable makeup cases, styling products and tools of beauty that instilled fear into most women, lay organized by the frequency of their use. The right side of the cabinet was all Julian. Shaver, spare toothbrushes, extra toilet paper. Very sparse indeed. But Julian the man was sparse; sparse in frame, sparse in manner, sparse of words. He pulled out the hot rollers and set them on the counter and plugged them in. He walked back into his room, and opted not to use the earphones he'd plugged into his laptop. He discarded them onto the bed. Instead, he cranked the volume in his control panel, to drown out the argument that continued below him, and hit 'Play'. The first refrains from "My Heart Will Go On" started, but Julian's hurt was too raw still to be able to listen to it, so he hit the fast forward button and continued to prepare, silently mouthing the words to "I Drove All Night" as it played.

Thirty minutes later, Julian was sitting back at his computer, still mouthing along to the words from the current song that played. He reached up and angled the mirror above his computer downwards so that when the urge struck him, he could glance up and dramatically sing to his reflection.

He had an avocado face mask on, and hot rollers adorned his head. He shuffled in his seat, pulled the robe around him and tightened the thin sash. He was pleasantly warm, having just pulled his body from a scalding bath. He rubbed his calves together where they crossed beneath his chair. There were few sensations in life that truly brought him joy (outside the bedroom, of course), but one of them was the feeling of freshly shaved and moisturized legs. He wiggled his toes in joy.

He had ten minutes before the mask needed to be washed away, but before he allowed himself to peruse his favorite online haunt, he had some business to take care of. He picked up the cordless phone next to his tabletop lamp, and quickly dialed from memory.

"Wolves Den", a harsh male voice answered.

Julian cleared his throat lightly, "Franco, please," his voice automatically rising and softening as 'Julia' became more and more pronounced.

"Hang on." Julian was unceremoniously placed on hold, and while he was waiting he inspected his hairline in the mirror. He grimaced slightly at the Muzak that wailed in his ear.

"Franco here." The line snapped to life.

"Franco? It's Julia. Julia NewMar. How are you, darling?"

"Julia!" Franco sounded genuinely surprised, "we haven't seen you around this way in quite some time. I heard that you had been whisked away to Saskatchewan, or some such place, to sing for some cowboys. They let you out of their lassos long enough for you to get back to the Big Apple did they?"

"It was Quebec, darling," Julia turned up the saccharine in her voice, not allowing any emotion to show. "And you should know better than to believe every rumor you hear." Julia admonished, "I've been in the city all along, just slightly ... out of commission."

"Well now that you're back, or should I say, now that you're back in commission, what can I do for you? Are you back on the stage as well?"

"Well, Franco, of course you were the first person I thought of, but yes. I'm back with a vengeance. And I want to sing. Tonight. Can you squeeze me in?"

"For you, Julia? Anything. I'll make room. Can you be here by nine?"

Julia paused to keep her tone in check. *Nine?* Did Franco think she was a goddamned *amateur* or something? Next, he'd have her on stage first, while the clientele were still being served their first drinks! Julia paused, keeping her voice in check. "Of course. Did you really say 'nine'?"

"I won't be able to pay you, ya know – as a last minute booking, I'll be cutting back on another queen's time. There'll be hell to pay, but for you I'm willing to take the flak."

"I knew I could count on you Franco, that's why you're the first person I called tonight." She paused dramatically, "I'll bring my own music – ah, Franco? How many pieces should I bring?" Say three you bloody greedy bastard, say three.

"Two for sure, but bring a third just in case we can squeeze it in."

"Fabulous." Julia crooned, and could almost see Franco counting the extra 'take'. Anytime she performed, drink specials flew out of the bar. She was a draw, and tonight she'd be a surprise. "I'll see you at nine, Franco. Kisses."

She rang off before Franco could say his own smarmy good byes.

Julia replaced the telephone on its cradle, and in doing so, Julian returned and spun slightly to face his computer. Right, he thought, that accomplished, I have one more task before I can really get started. He called up Julia's email account, goddessinmyownmind@gmail.com, and quickly composed a crucial email. It read:

> Friends, Lovers, Queens, and my Adoring Fans,
>
> I HAVE RETURNED.
>
> Tonight. After 9pm. Wolves Den. Be there or force me to track you down and rake a manicured fingertip or two somewhere decidedly unpleasant.
>
> Wear your party pumps girls! You know I will be!
>
> In celebration, I might just let you buy me a drink or two...
>
> Kisses,
>
> Julia

With a quick click of his touch pad, Julian opened up the address book stored in Yahoo. He quickly found the group he was looking for and placed a check mark next to 'Party People'. Once the lengthy list of names was added to the email, he pressed the send button, and sat back with a satisfied sigh. Wheels were officially in motion. He knew that all around the city, with just that one click of a button, queens and fag hags alike were scurrying around, changing plans and outfits in order to prepare for the spectacle to be played out at the Wolves Den. He wriggled his nose and grimaced slightly. The mask that was supposed to moisturize and tone his skin had become uncomfortably tight. Once again, he stood from his computer and headed to the bathroom to let the real transformation from Julian to Julia begin.

∞

Julia glanced at the thin gold-banded watch that lay around her delicate wrist. It has been too long, she thought to herself as she fastened the clasp. This should never have taken two hours. She was now bordering on being late for her return to the stage. The perfectionist in her was screaming for the diva in her to hurry. The diva was winning the battle of time, yelling back, "Let them wait! They've waited four months for this night, they can wait another hour. I'll make it worth their while. I always do!"

Watch fastened, Julia leaned as far into the full-length mirror as she dared. She was annoyed to see that her hands shook slightly, and that annoyance quickly turned to being appalled at herself. She was Julia NewMar. She didn't get ... nervous. She hadn't had stage fright since before the first time she took the stage half a decade before. She managed one earring without harming herself, and jabbed her ear painfully with the second stud before successfully attaching it to her lobe.

Julia closed her eyes, took a step back from the mirror, and inhaled a deep cleansing breath, bringing her ring-laden fingers to her breast. And another breath, visualizing her heart slowing its furious pace. And another, and another, until she felt her heartbeat return to its normal strong beat. She brought her hands, steady once more, down to her sides, and straightened herself up to her 6'1" height. She slowly opened her eyes, and the sight that was revealed made her smile widely. Her hair was coiffed impeccably, her makeup was flawless, the dress clung in all the right places and flowed generously where it should. Her toned legs were sheathed in the finest silk hose, and on her feet were the shoes that made the outfit.

Julia's eyes roamed up and down her form. Yes ... *Yes!* She was back, and she was ready. She struck a pose, and it made her smile. Just for the fun of it, she struck another. Indeed the fortunate patrons at the bar tonight were in for a special treat. She was in rare form, and she looked fabulous.

She took her chosen purse from where it hung with a selection of others behind the door, and surveyed what was inside. She quickly crossed into the bathroom and placed additional essential items into her handbag. Foundation, liner, lipstick, gloss, mascara, pocket-sized hairspray, all managed to be crammed into the little leather bag. Feeling a confidence that had been lacking even ten minutes prior, Julia left her bedroom, and headed down the hall towards the stairs.

Her heels echoed on each hardwood stair as she walked down into the foyer. Her parents, still arguing, were now in the sitting room. Julia could see that her father was sitting in his chair reading the paper and her mother was on the sofa doing some mending. Julia was amazed that they could be completely engrossed in other things but still be bickering with each other. They didn't pause as Julia crossed in front of the open French doors that were the entranceway into the sitting room. But as she grabbed her keys from the hook beside the front door, her mother's voice echoed across the heavy wood panels. "Have a good show tonight, Julia."

Julia smiled to herself as she locked the front door behind her, crossing into the early summer evening.

FOUR

LUCINDA LOGGED onto the Manolo Blahnik website and forums as if it were second nature. With her administrative password, it was a snap to find herself behind the scenes, and anonymous to the posting crowd. She'd done this before on a Saturday night, and as she scanned the list of posters online wished she'd thought of this days ago. The same old faithful clientele were online tonight. No one new. No one to play with, no one's brain to pick.

For just a moment, Lucinda contemplated creating a new persona, with a name no one could suspect was her. She dismissed this idea almost as quickly as it entered her mind. The amount of energy that was needed as a newbie to the board, the saccharine pleasantries and introductions with these people she understood so well could be put to better use. She adjusted the pillow behind her back, pulled the duvet over her crossed legs, and with a precise click of her mouse, made herself visible to the posting world.

Response was immediate. And the creation of a private chat room seemed instantaneous. Lucinda knew these posters were 'old school fans' of Manolo, back when he was just a lone designer in Milan, risking everything on each design of each shoe. These people were the backbone of the company. They were why Lucinda had a job. They knew Manolo's shoes better than some of the employees themselves. They studied Manolo Blahnik, they'd mastered his design. Lucinda loved them for their dedication through good designs and bad, but rather sneered at them for their blind adoration, for not seeing that Manolo was just a man not a god, that he sat on the toilet and scratched his balls, just like anyone else.

She shook her head and refocused on the invitation to chat that had appeared on her screen. Once she clicked on the 'accept' button, she was tied in to this chat for the remainder of the evening. She'd made the mistake before, of hoping to pop online for a few minutes before a meeting, or just before she was due to head home. There seemed to be a minimum time requirement when you chatted with these people, and it registered in hours, not minutes.

Lucinda accepted the chat invitation and steeled herself for the barrage that was due to be pelted her way.

DDDWide: Good Lord Almity, ISYS wtf are you doing here?

ChatInSole: :: waves isys a warm welcome ::

Spike: Yo, Isys, you've been missed girl! WB.

Thi-Hi-Hooer: have you come back to kick some royal MB Ass???????

ISYS: Thanks for the welcome, ladies! It has been too long.

DDDWide: I dunno Isys, this leaving us hanging for months at a time is growing old!

Spike: :: smacks DDD ::

DDDWide: Ouch!

Spike: Deserved that.

ISYS: I know, I know, and actually, I deserve that smack DDD. I have been gone too long, and I did leave things hanging last time.

ChatInSole: ISYS, we know you're busy. You're welcome here anytime you have a free moment.

DDDWide: CIS, you are a suck up.

> *Thi-Hi-Hooer:* SNORT!
>
> *Spike:* *grabs garden hose and sprays down the complainers*
>
> *ChatInSole:* DDD you are full of piss and vinegar tonight, what's your problem? On the rag?
>
> *Thi-Hi-Hooer:* DDD spent her alimony check this week on that new pair of midnight blue strappy sandals that was shipped out last week and they've cut off the circulation to her brain. LOL
>
> *DDD Wide:* You can kiss my black as night but still spectacular ass.
>
> *Spike:* I tried on those sandals and they didn't quite fit my insole, but in general, I liked 'em fine.
>
> *Thi-Hi-Hooer:* You'd like shit if it had rhinestones on it and a four hundred dollar price tag Spike.
>
> *Spike:* Bitch.
>
> *Thi-Hi-Hooer:* Whore.
>
> *ChatInSole:* Cat fight!!

Lucinda sighed. This was the one downside to doing work like this in a chat room. Drama. There was always some sort of drama going on. If you liked the shoes too much you were a suck. If you didn't like the shoes, then what the hell were you doing in a Manolo Blahnik chat room to begin with? Lucinda could feel her sanity slipping away as the 'War of Words' raged on the screen in front of her. She slipped off the bed and headed into the kitchen. Grabbing a bottle of water from the fridge and a granola bar from the cupboard above the stove, she took her fuel back into the bedroom. As she passed her purse on the counter, she took a quick glance at her cell phone.

Yep, one missed call. She didn't check to see who it was. She had a feeling she knew. Hank could suck it. She wasn't going to appease his guilty conscience tonight. She erased the message without listening to it, dropped the cell back into her purse with disdain and continued back to the bedroom.

The battle had escalated while she'd been gone. Lucinda scrolled up a bit to catch up, hoping that someone somewhere had decided to actually put on screen what was the issue with that particular style of shoe and its lack of comfort. She wasn't in luck.

Although tonight Lucinda was in no mood for the drama – she'd had enough in her world as of late – she usually took secret pleasure in reading the scathing insults that tended to fly like dust in a windstorm in these chat rooms. She had even had opportunity to use a couple of them in her day to day dealings: thank you, Thi-Hi, Lucinda thought. One insult had been incredibly effective, leaving its victim a pooling mass in the coffee room. Lucinda smiled, remembering the bumbling intern who had fallen victim to her slash. The intern's welling eyes, the bottom lip that quivered, and as Lucinda delivered the deathblow, the tears that fell. Lucinda had left the poor intern to mop up for herself.

Tonight, however, she was all business, and wanted to get the information she needed and get out. Waiting for a lull in the insults, Lucinda primed the questions she was going to pose. After a few moments, she typed:

> *ISYS:* So ladies, it's great to catch up but I do have a question for you.
>
> *DDD Wide:* See arse-wipe we got bettr things to talk about. Whazzup isis
>
> *ChatInSole:* Shoot

> *Thi-Hi-Hooer:* #yawn#

Lucinda smiled at Thi-Hi's lack of interest.

> *ISYS:* I could have instant messaged you all individually, but figure this would kill 2 birds w/ one stone

Lucinda let a dramatic pause play out.

> *ISYS:* Do you think there are any MEN on this board who are masquerading as women – just to get the skinny on the shoes?

Again, there was a pregnant pause as the chatters processed the question. Then the comments that showed up on Lucinda's computer screen came fast and furious.

> *DDDWide:* BWAAHAAH! WWHAAHAAHAAA!
>
> *ChatInSole:* ddd
>
> *Thi-Hi-Hooer:* DDD
>
> *ChatInSole:* u think i joke?
>
> *Thi-Hi-Hooer:* good one chat!
>
> *DDDWide:* bitches!
>
> *ChatInSole:* great minds Thi
>
> *DDDWide:* shut da f up!! y'all dont no what your starting...
>
> *ChatInSole:* i always knew your voice was deep, ddd
>
> *Thi-Hi-Hooer:* gonna kick my ass with your size 12 shoe?
>
> *DDDWide:* if I could get out to Long Island I would ya hole.
>
> *Thi-Hi-Hooer:* you could try, but i'm skinny, i move fast

> *DDDWide:*   u can't run far enough or fast enough skunk nugget.
>
> *ChatInSole:* LOL thi
>
> *ISYS:* I'm completely serious
>
> *ChatInSole:* SO was I...
>
> *Thi-Hi-Hooer:* me to
>
> *DDDWide:* Skankwads all of you
>
> *ISYS:* you all have been regulars on this site since i've been coming here, but you know more posters than I do.

Lucinda's fingers flew across her keyboard.

> ISYS: I'm just curious.
>
> *DDDWide:* curiosity killed a feline or two in its time isys
>
> *DDDWide:* why do you think some cross dressing queen would come out to us
>
> *ISYS:* because DDD you have a way of extracting info that I don't

Lucinda didn't mind lying. After all these months, the posters who knew of ISYS thought that she was a shoe buyer in New York. No one had ever asked her who she was working for, and no one questioned her quest for information, nor had they pried into her job, potentially calling her bluff. Because she was unquestioningly accepted as someone with 'inside information' into the shoe world, she was considered somewhat of an expert, even revered by a few of the posters.

In truth, Lucinda could easily look in the Manolo Blahnik database, the one compiled from each of the outlets, and have looked into which men were purchasing. With every pair of shoes sold, a zip code was required to complete the sale. But Lucinda wasn't dumb: she knew that if she were a cross-dresser, she'd be purchasing online, not at a storefront, and she would use an alias. That made her search more difficult as one person could use numerous aliases. A zip code was still needed to mail out the shoes, but zip codes were unisexual.

> *DDDWide:* I can't think of anyone off the top of my head
>
> *ChatInSole:* hang on...
>
> *Thi-Hi-Hooer:* are you thinking of who i'm thinking of chat?
>
> *ChatInSole:* Julia
>
> *Thi-Hi-Hooer:* Julia

Lucinda reached behind her and opened the small drawer in her nightstand, extracting the small booklet and pen that accompanied it. Both had been sitting exactly where she'd left them. She dutifully wrote 'Julia' at the top of a clean page.

> *DDDWide:* Julia?
>
> *Thi-Hi-Hooer:* yeah, you know, QueenoftheEffingUniverse

Lucinda almost choked on the water she'd just sipped. What a fabulous screen name! Why the *hell* hadn't she thought of it first! She scrawled the screen name under 'Julia' in her notebook and underlined it. Twice.

> *Thi-Hi-Hooer:* get with the program ddd
>
> *ChatInSole:* you didnt know, ddd?
>
> *DDDWide:* how could i not know that

> *Thi-Hi-Hooer:* cause you wear yor shoes too tight, sweetie
>
> *ChatInSole:* yer head is so far up your own butt you couldnt see daylight, ddd

Lucinda wanted to keep this on track, so the insults wouldn't take over the chat again, thus wasting her time.

> *ISYS:* before the bitch fest starts again...
>
> *ISYS:* does Julia come here often
>
> *ChatInSole:* haven't seen her/him in a while
>
> *DDDWide:* i saw her online a couple of weeks ago but she's been scarce
>
> *Thi-Hi-Hooer:* HE, ddd
>
> *DDDWide:* whaddevah, loser
>
> *Thi-Hi-Hooer:* no sightings, ISYS

Lucinda sighed. She could see hours of research into the online database in front of her. Then she shook her head, and grinned. The next intern to piss her off would be given the tedious task. She cackled lightly to herself.

> *ISYS:* Ok
>
> *ISYS:* if you speak with her online anytime over the next little while ask her to instant message me, or personal message me, k?
>
> *ChatInSole:* you bet
>
> *DDDWide:* sure
>
> *Thi-Hi-Hooer:*k

> *DDDWide:* you aren't leaving are you isys? We need your expert opinion.
>
> *ChatInSole:* don't go yet

Lucinda smiled and opened the wrapper on her granola bar and snapped off a small piece, popping it into her mouth.

> *ISYS:* na. Not yet. I've missed you guys
>
> *ChatInSole:* :: yay!::
>
> *Thi-Hi-Hooer:* excellent
>
> *DDDWide:* good, because we are due some good dirt. You owe us
>
> *ChatInSole:* and i have questions about the new autumn line coming out
>
> *ISYS:* I'm all yours. Fire away...

Having started the ball rolling with this new research project, Lucinda sat back, lifted her laptop so it rested on her bent knees, and answered all the questions she could as these loyal customers typed them out. She did so quite happily. Sometimes entertainment could be found in the most mundane activities, and after all it was folks like this who paid Lucinda's more-than-decent salary.

∞

Oliver sat at his desk, leaned back in his chair, crossed his legs delicately and found his toe tapping the air to the beat of 'Waterloo' that echoed from his bedroom. Despite the unexpected change in his plans, Oliver was having a fabulous evening. He had wine, he looked fabulous, and his goddess, his muse in shoes had made an appearance at his favorite on-

line haunt. ISYS. She was back and she was asking some
interesting questions.

Oliver still considered himself an internet plebeian, although
he would never admit that to anyone, online or in person.
When he had arranged cable internet service to his apartment,
he had thought he would only be using it to download stock
information, or to pay bills online. Little did he know that
he would be able to indulge in his wildest fantasies so
anonymously.

Three years ago, after a particularly harsh break up, Oliver
had decided to venture into the world of internet dating. While
scoping a few decidedly unappealing personals, a pop-up
ad had caught his attention and he was hooked. In blazing
color, with flashing bold lettering before him, was the most
wonderful advertisement for women's shoes. Oliver's eyes
had dilated, and he started to salivate. Even his finger shook
slightly as he moved his cursor over the ad and clicked. His
world had been forever altered.

The site had been for a discount shoe outlet, offering
amazing deals due to online purchasing power (and probably
selling last season's 'overs' too boot). Oliver had spent hours,
clear into the wee part of the morning, ogling the different
styles and colors available. And that's when he'd seen them,
his pride and joy. He'd fallen in love. His black patent leather
pumps, the ones that adorned his feet as he sat and typed, had
been his first and only online womens' shoe purchase.

From that evening on, after a vicious day at work or a
particularly tedious call from Mama, Oliver could be found
sitting in the glow of his computer monitor, his legs sheathed
in silk, his feet shod in his tried and true patent leather pumps,
investigating each and every shoe website he could find via

Google. Jimmy Choo, BGBC, Kenneth Cole, 9 West and countless others. None had been above scrutiny. He loved Google for the world that had been opened up to him. When he had stumbled upon the Manolo Blahnik site, initially he had passed it by, thinking that his trusty Google had made an error. Who was Manolo Blahnik, and why would he have a site listed under a search for 'shoes + women'? So he'd skipped by it on that first night, and on many after that.

He'd always credited Google for his introduction to Manolo Blahnik, but in truth, it was Anne Cole. It was a link that was located on her shoe site; one Oliver had clicked on in error, that had brought Manolo Blahnik the shoe designer to his full attention. And when the slick website had popped up on his computer, with its stylized Italian script and single rotating four inch heeled pump of fabulousness focused in a spotlight in the centre of the main page, Oliver's breath caught in his throat. He felt he had reached his Nirvana.

He had taken hour after blissful hour scrutinizing every aspect of the website. He'd pored over the inventory listed on their 'Store' page. He'd signed up for their email newsletter which he devoured each month it was delivered to a secret email inbox.

At the bottom corner of the third email newsletter he received, there was a small article and link that had announced the instigation of 'The Manolo Blahnik Message Board – a place to discuss, obsess, and scrutinize the shoe designs of a Milanese Master'.

Oliver lurked through his first six months at the Manolo Blahnik message board. The posters left him in awe, and they intimidated the hell out of him. How they knew as much as they did boggled his mind. And about the shoes! You would think they had been researching spending $400,000 on a custom-built Masserati, not $600 on a pair of pumps. These shoe aficionados knew dimensions, color shades and thread colours; they knew the difference in stitching from one shoe to the next. They amazed him with the scope of their knowledge.

Oliver had been afraid at first, afraid that he wouldn't be able to pull off the charade of his inexperience and most of all his sex. But after a few tentative posts, and some good natured, and some not so good natured ribbing about his lack of shoe knowledge (he'd played ignorant to the difference between a slingback and a mule), he had fit in quite well with the other posters.

And he learned. He'd made friends and he'd inadvertently made enemies. He'd been a regular at the Manolo Blahnik website for the last three years, and he loved it. He could be whoever he wanted to be. He could be exactly who he felt he was. There were no judgments as no one there really knew him at all. And that was all part of the appeal. He was anonymous. He was DDDWide.

FIVE

JULIA WAS a convincing woman. She was tall, with legs that seemed to end at her armpits, and she dressed – albeit tonight a bit dressier than other women wandering through the streets of New York City – with class. And she appeared to be "built", no matter how artificial it all was. She got double glances from taxi drivers. She even got a couple of wolf whistles from men walking on the opposite side of the street.

This made her smile. She hadn't lost it, the appeal, even after all these months of being away from the life. Julia revelled in the attention, almost more than when she was on stage, as the audience inevitably knew they were going to experience the best drag show of their lives. These unsuspecting men on the street had no clue that they were wasting their testosterone on one of their own kind – on one of their own sex. This successful deception thrilled her.

Julia rapped her knuckles quickly on the back door of the Wolves Den. When no one immediately answered, she let herself in. She met Louis, the brawny bouncer, as she made her way up the dark hall towards the dressing rooms. They greeted each other with the familiarity of old friends. With a quick peck on both cheeks, Julia paused to catch up a bit.

"Well, Louis? Who's throwing a tantrum tonight?"

"Jules, I for one am glad you're back You are a calm queen – not like the bitches we've had in here lately. Demanding, emotional, jeez, you'd think they were all hormonal." He amended his last statement, "Well Babs actually *is* hormonal. She's started her treatment."

"Get out! When? Ugh, I wish I'd known, I would have brought her some chocolate or Tampax or something," Julia said with a smile. Her tone was slightly catty, and she knew it.

"I dunno, a couple of weeks ago?" Louis sighed, "It's beyond me." He shrugged nonchalantly, "To each her own?"

Julia winked and laid a delicate hand on Louis' beefy forearm, "You've got that right, sugar. But don't worry; I'll go calm the wenches down. Tonight is going to be a show to remember."

Louis laughed roughly and started backing up towards the door, "Good luck tonight, Julia. The gals aren't that pleased you're back to steal their thunder. Be aware and watch your back."

"I would expect no less from those wannabes. Tonight I'm going to give them something to aspire to."

"I don't doubt that, Julia. Not in the slightest. Oh, and watch out for Franco. He's pissed you're late for your first night back."

Julia wiggled her fingers to him in a good-bye wave and turned to make her way to the dressing rooms, cursing herself. It was unprofessional and diva-ish to be late for a performance. Julia stole a glance at the watch on her wrist. It was only quarter past. It wasn't like she had held up the show or anything. The newcomers, new either to queendom or to performing, usually went on stage first. Julia grimaced. If Franco was really pissed, he might put her on with them. That would be worse than insulting. Faced with a 'T' in the hallway, she opted to pre-empt any dramatics that may occur in the dressing rooms to her left, and decided to take the stairs to the office on her right instead. She'd come groveling back, so she might as well make the experience complete and go apologize, rectifying whatever slight to Franco prior to her performance tonight.

Julia had no trouble finding Franco's office. She knocked delicately, and when the bark echoed out for her to come in, Julia took pause for a moment, putting a saccharine look on her face, and a subdued tone in her voice. She opened the door with a flourish.

"Franco, darling, I hope you weren't worried about me not showing."

Franco – balding, paunchy Franco – barely looked up from the stack of bills that littered his cluttered desk, "Humph."

"It was completely my fault. I take complete responsibility for my own tardiness. I wanted my hair to be exactly perfect for my first performance back at your club. You recall how much of a perfectionist I am. It reflects in my performance. And thus in your profits, no?"

At the mention of money, Franco's eyes snapped to Julia's.

"Julia, I'm glad you're back. Really. Truly. But don't be late again. You know it pisses me off."

"I know, I *know*, Franco, and I'm so terribly sorry. It won't happen again. You know my track record. I'm punctual to a fault – tonight was just a blip."

"Blip, yeah, whatever. Go get ready for your show. You're up after Saundra."

"Thanks Franco." Julia cooed as she turned the handle on the door and left.

Only when she made it several paces down the hall from his office did she complete her thought. Thanks for fucking nothing, Franco. After Saundra? *Saundra, for Christsake??* Yes, make me pay; make me pay for my sabbatical from performing. I was your cash cow for more years than you'd like to admit. Asshole.

Julia stopped dead in her tracks in the hallway and gave her head a little shake, causing the light curls she'd created to brush her cheeks. She made a conscious effort to ease the furrow in her brow. It amazed her how little remained of the defense she had built up over the years. Last year, she would never have let a petty bugger like Franco push her buttons. Ever. She pushed. Never the other way around. She continued her walk to the dressing rooms, and with each graceful, measured step, her calm and confidence returned.

She needed both. When she opened the door to the dressing room that was as familiar to her as her own bedroom, chaos erupted. Julia knew better than to believe the cries of welcome that threatened to overwhelm her. She knew that behind the kisses that were bestowed on her lightly blushed cheeks there were fangs that would cut her down in an instant given half a chance. She knew with each hug that was given, she was gripped with claws that would scratch out her eyes out if she weren't careful.

She accepted the welcome cautiously, and bantered back and forth with the ladies she had spent so much time with, and was introduced with much praise to a few newcomers. The newbies had all heard of Julia NewMar of course. Everyone had heard of Julia. And her abrupt departure from the stage had caused much rumor and speculation – some of which, Julia was sure, was started by Franco himself in hopes of adding to his own pocketbook.

Only one person remained in the background, waiting for the barrage of greetings to run its course. Sophia. Sophia, the Mama hen to all queens who took to the stage of the Wolves Den. Sophia, who had known Julia prior to Julian knowing Julia. Sophia, who had helped create Julia, and in the process became both friend and confidante. Julia felt those heavily eyelashed eyes on her, searching through the babble of greeting for hidden threats and dangers. As their eyes met across the room, it was clear that Sophia's eyes showed genuine love, real pleasure, without the slightest iota of resentment.

It was into Sophia's arms that Julia found herself passed at long last. The chubby arms of her mentor passed about Julia's slim frame, and Julia found herself nuzzled in the ample bosom of the Queen of all Queens. Whereas Julia was well known, Sophia was a positive legend in the drag community in New York. Julia was pulled out of the embrace and was held away at arms length.

"Let me look at you." Sophia instructed.

While Sophia circled, inspecting Julia's outfit, makeup and hair, Julia allowed herself to dissect Sophia. She's aged, Julia thought, she's gotten heavier. Julia's eyes did a full-on inspection. Famous blonde beehive wig and heavily overdone makeup seemed to fit Sophia's persona to a tee – as did the gaudy mumu that she wore. It was heavily inspired by the 60's, and white vinyl boots rounded out the ensemble. So it was going to be a Nancy Sinatra kind of night for Sophia, who always, always sat backstage and watched each performance, only taking the stage herself to close the show. It was always a rousing success. Sophia routinely stole the show, and although there had been a point where Julia was exceedingly jealous of the matriarch's power and prestige, it was always overshadowed by the love that the two of them shared. It was a love that is often shared between teacher and student, for in fact, Sophia had helped the then Julian discover Julia. Julia had been coached on style, makeup, walking in heels. Sophia had taken Julian in completely, and Julia had sashayed out. It was a close relationship.

"You've grown too thin, ma chere," Sophia crooned, turning Julia in another half circle. "You haven't lost it completely during your sojourn, though. That's good. But if you are in fact coming back to performing, we need to meet and I'll give you some of the new inside information."

Julia nodded respectfully, "I appreciate any and all wisdom you can throw my way, Sophia. You know that."

"Yes, indeed I do know." Sophia grinned, but there was a mysterious glint in her eye.

She dropped her hands to her side from where they had been resting on Julia's shoulders. Her head tilted slightly, in an expression that Julia recognized immediately as a critique. Sophia thought for a moment, then pulled Julia over to the heavily lit make up table and physically sat her down, spinning her in the process towards the mirror.

"Julia, Julia, Julia. Did you forget everything while you were away? What in heaven's name have you done to your hair? You look like you've just walked in out of a wind storm."

"You still aren't mincing words are you, Soph." Julia smiled at the reflection of her mentor.

"Honey, we don't have time for pleasantries. We have a show to prepare for!"

The dressing room emptied as performers went out to watch other acts. When Sophia was about half way through working her magic, Julia felt the old panic return momentarily, and brought a hand to her stomach in hopes of quelling her sudden flight of butterflies. Sophia stopped bobby pinning and laid one hand on Julia's where it pressed against her midriff.

"It's natural, you know – to feel nervous."

"I don't get nervous, Soph. I never have, so what is this feeling now? I belong on stage. We both know that. What is this in my gut? Have I made a mistake coming back?"

"Do you want to be here tonight?"

"Of course."

"Would you do anything to perform?"

"Other than giving Franco a blow job, yes."

Sophia's bosom jiggled as she laughed, "Well, honey, it hasn't come to that yet." Sophia continued with bobby pinning Julia's hair about the crown of the head. "But trust in Sophia as you did seven years ago when we met. You are meant for the stage. Trust in yourself."

"Thanks Sophia, I feel better."

"Of course you do," Sophia muttered, sticking the last pin into the up-coif that Celine herself would have been proud of,

"I have deemed it so." And with a wink, Sophia ushered Julia out towards the stage.

Julia made a bee-line to the DJ when she reached backstage. She handed him the CD she'd tucked in her purse last minute. "Tracks 3, 1, then 6 please."

"When you on?" came a gruff response.

"After Saundra."

"You're Julia, huh. I've heard about you."

Julia just smiled graciously, batted her eyelashes and turned towards the stage.

When Saundra, with her usual dramatic flair, exited into the wings after her performance, Julia felt a familiar jump in heart rate. She was nervous no longer; she was pumped with adrenaline. She was excited.

There was a rousing response to her introduction. And when she walked slowly through the center curtains onto the stage and felt the first heat of the spotlight in her face, and roar of applause ringing in her ears, Julia felt a peace she hadn't known in months. She had come home.

SIX

IT WAS after one a.m. when Lucinda finally hit the shut down button on her laptop. She stretched luxuriously, easing out the kink that had found its way between her shoulder blades. She rolled her neck slowly, easing each ear down to her shoulders, then rolled it back the other way, and made a mental note not to do this sort of chatting again while she was sitting on her bed. She had the best of mattresses that money could buy, but it was more conducive to a restful sleep rather than tucking up and chatting with cyber clients. Her chiropractor would have his work cut out for him a week Tuesday, when she was due for her next appointment.

As she swung her legs off her bed, her spine cracked so loudly it startled her. Monday, she said to herself. I need to change that appointment to this Monday. Her brain automatically rearranged the next couple of days, as if meetings and schedules were as compact as a Tetris game. It took a few minutes, but the end result was a timetable that would leave the hour and a half span between 3:30 and 5:00 on Monday open for Dr Warshinsk.

Lucinda had no worries about changing the meetings she'd need to at the office. When Lucinda MacHauley said that the meeting was being postponed or pushed forward, you agreed or you risked being served your own head on a platter.

The same went for Dr Warshinsk. He'd squeeze her in even if he didn't have an opening available. He always did. Lucinda grabbed the wrapper from her consumed granola bar and the empty water bottle, and headed out of her bedroom.

Lucinda relished the overwhelming, almost stifling silence that accompanied these early morning hours in New York City. These were her favorite hours of the 24-hour clock, when the local bars weren't yet closed and the streets were still relatively quiet. As Lucinda left her bedroom and headed towards the kitchen, she shut the window in the living room that had been letting in a pleasant spring breeze.

A taxi horn blared loudly from stories below her, but it echoed up the side of her building so it reached her almost at full volume. She jumped uncharacteristically. It must be later than she thought, as a second horn blast reached her window. Yes, people would be pouring themselves, and perhaps a playmate for the night, out of bars and into taxis to get their intoxicated selves home. Lucinda smiled to herself, remembering how close she had become to being one of those people tonight. She'd had a productive evening of a different sort, even if it didn't involve any leather play.

Having secured the latch on the window, and pulled the shades tightly closed, Lucinda finally wove her way into her dimly lit kitchen. She tipped the water bottle into the recycling bin underneath the kitchen sink and tossed the wrapper into the garbage. She straightened herself and was caught unawares by something sitting just above the sink. It was something that had managed to miss her earlier anti-Hank cleansing of the apartment.

She reached up and picked up the handmade paper card, her fingertips tracing the simple black Japanese symbol painted directly onto the front. She felt tears start to well, and cursed herself. She must be tired if she found sentimentality in a piece of card stock. But even with that thought, she flipped the card open and read the contents. She smiled a bittersweet smile and read it again.

" *Lucy,*" The card began,

You are the solar flare that throws my magnets out of whack.

You are the steel that can't be bent.

You are the gale that tosses my ship.

You are the light that leads me home.

I adore you. Don't ever change.

Love, Hank

No one had ever written Lucinda a poem before. No one had taken the time. Lucinda had little time for poetry. Flowery words did thought a disservice; just say what you mean when the situation arises. To Lucinda, cards were a sickly sweet invention used to convey Christmas sentiment, or perhaps a birthday salutation; they were a waste. Email was cheaper, not that money was an issue. But time always was in Lucinda's world, so if firing off an e-card was far more time efficient, firing off an e-card was what Lucinda did. She wasn't impolite, just perhaps impersonal. It was easier keeping everything at a distance. Even Hank.

Hank knew Lucy, not Lucinda. He accepted the bitchy workaholic Lucinda the outside world saw, but he was falling for Lucy, the girl he'd met in high school and just happened to bump into at a restaurant years later. On more than one occasion she'd allowed him to strip off, not just her clothes, but the hard shell of Lucinda. He truly saw her, and that scared the shit out of her. She closed the card and traced the rough edges with her forefinger absentmindedly. What was she to do with this card? A very small part of her wanted to throw it away, just as she had the toothbrush and deodorant. Just as she had Hank. With renewed strength, Lucinda whipped open the cupboard beneath the sink and shoved the card underneath. But her hand refused to release the card into the gaping void of the paper recycling bag. Instead, Lucinda found she wanted to keep it, and this realization surprised her. So she shuffled back towards her bedroom, turning out the lights of the rooms she passed through.

She stood in front of her dresser for several minutes before she could bring herself to open up the top left-hand drawer. Underneath some implements of perversion that she brought out on special occasions – more often than not those occasions had been with Hank – she placed the card face down under a leather blindfold. She closed the drawer firmly, not wanting to think of that part of her life tonight. She rolled her neck again stiffly, the collar of her old flannel night gown suddenly feeling like it was strangling her.

She hauled the cloth over her head, and tossed the discarded garment onto the floor of her closet. She couldn't be Lucy any longer. It was a place of rawness, or emotion, and she wasn't comfortable there any longer. In her nakedness, where she should have felt more exposed than ever, Lucinda found her strength, her 'steel' as Hank put it. And it was with strength that Lucinda lay down, still bare, her king size bed dwarfing her even further, and she allowed herself to relax into a slumber devoid of dreams of shoes and leather as she worried the leather band that surrounded her wrist.

∞

Oliver was in awe of ISYS. She knew everything and had her finger firmly on the pulse of the footwear world. She had intimidated the bejeezus out of him when they had first come in contact; so much so that when ISYS had joined a chat room where DDDWide and several other clients were debating the pros and cons of rhinestones versus diamondettes, DDDWide had stopped chatting altogether. In those early days, Oliver preferred to watch ISYS in action, rather than banter with her directly. And ultimately the online persona that he had chosen had been based on ISYS, though the details of him living in Yonkers, being African American, and, oh, the small one of him being a woman – well those were his own. The attitude had come directly, 100% from ISYS. Oliver smiled as he followed the familiar routine of shutting down his computer. His apartment was silent; the ABBA CDs that rotated around his Bang & Olafsen system and were the soundtrack for this evening's chat had run their course hours ago. Now, Oliver welcomed the silence. He still had echoes of cyber voices running around his head.

He allowed his imagination free reign when he tried to envision the voice of ChatInSole. Hers would be a voice of higher range, slightly strained after yelling at her lazy, unemployed husband and three disgracefully lazy children all day. She'd been introduced to Manolo Blahnik through 'Sex in the City', and had made it a life goal to own one pair of Blahnik shoes. She hadn't found them yet, but she'd confided early on that she took $10 out of the family food budget each month so she could tuck it away and purchase her dream shoes when she found them. She was still looking, and Oliver had serious doubts as to whether any shoe would ever measure up to the design that ChatInSole had in her middle-class mind.

What about Thi-Hi-Hooer? Well, she would have Long Island down pat. She was all about the boots, and would spend as much of her small disposable income as she could on a 'good' pair of boots. Oliver pictured her growing up in a low-income family, where your school shoes were your play shoes were your gym shoes. There would have been no such thing as disposable income, and quite often, Thi-Hi-Hooer had worn hand-me-shoes from her sister, who was older by two years. Even as a child, Thi had probably sworn that when she grew up, she would never, ever be stuck without shoes that made her proud to walk down the street. When she married well, she thought her dreams had come true, that her husband's income could provide stability for them and shoes for her. Two months after they wed, however, the marriage ended when her husband not only lost his job but then had a minor coronary upon opening the first visa bill that held record of an amazing four pairs of Manolo Blahniks purchased at a single boutique over a single weekend.

And Spike? Well, Spike was a bit of an anomaly in Manolo Blahnik's message board. Whereas Oliver usually allowed DDDWide to make an appearance late in the evening and was almost guaranteed to appear on a Friday or Saturday night, there was no rhyme or reason to Spike sightings. Oliver could only surmise two scenarios: either Spike was a 9-5er whose work place had no restrictions on where their employees roamed on the internet during work hours, or Spike was a Yuppie stay-at-home wife, who, after seeing her husband off with a peck on the cheek, had hours and hours at her disposal to peruse ways of spending her husband's money – in between yoga classes, that is.

Oliver plunked himself down on the edge of his bed. He contemplated doing the quick walk over to his CD player so that ABBA could serenade the routine that concluded the ruse of his evening, but he quickly decided against it. There were only rare moments of complete silence in Oliver's world, and he reveled in them when they occurred. He took a deep breath, and closed his eyes, blocking out the chat from the evening that was replaying in his mind. He leaned down and gently caressed the delicate fish net at his calf, running his hand from ankle to knee and back again. He reached down further and slipped the patent leather pump from his foot. He wiggled his toes, immediately missing the tight binding leather. The same ritual was repeated with his other foot. Oliver delicately placed both shoes, side by side, next to where his stockinged feet splayed on the carpet. He separated his robe from where it lay overlapped on his knees. He allowed one side to fall away, revealing his thigh and the lace trim of the fishnet stay-up stocking. He slipped his thumbs underneath where the elastic clung to the fine hairs on his leg. Gingerly, he stretched the elastic, and eased the stocking down. Slowly he dragged the fish net lower until, with one final light tug, he was free from its encasing. Oliver placed the stocking on the bed next to where he sat, then proceeded to do the same with his other leg.

Oliver smiled to himself as he looked down at the two deflated 'legs' that lay beside him on the duvet. The image reminded him of the Wicked Witch of the West from 'The Wizard of Oz' when Dorothy's house smashed down onto her, leaving her lifeless, poking out from underneath Dorothy's house. He delicately gathered them together by the toes, and folded them over onto each other. With a sigh he got up off the bed and crossed to the closet, released both the catches on the suitcase, and flipped the lid open. He unzipped the compartment that was in the lid of the case, and gingerly slipped the folded stockings into the pouch. He zipped the compartment back up, lowered the lid of the case, and secured the latches, double checking them just in case. His back cracked lightly as he hoisted the case over his head and put it back into the space it had vacated only hours before. Oliver ceremoniously closed his closet, obscuring the case from view, and stood for a moment, head bowed. He rocked on the balls of his feet, and with his hands on his hips, rolled his torso in a wide circle, hoping to release the tension that hung between his shoulder blades. Time to make a chiropractor appointment, he thought to himself as he padded towards the bathroom.

He shuffled his box to one side, leaving a wide enough berth so that any splash from the faucet wouldn't threaten the cardboard. Satisfied, he flipped the flaps open and with ease pulled out the makeup remover he'd purchased so long ago. The bottle was nearly empty, and he reflected on the uncomfortable minutes he had spent at the makeup counter at Macy's looking at different brands, not knowing one from the other, and having an awkward exchange with one of the salesladies when he finally got up the nerve to ask. He had stumbled over his words as he made the excuse of needing to purchase it for his own mother, and although the sales girl had looked at him slightly askance, she had directed him to this one brand. He had paid far too much, he was sure, and hadn't waited for the clerk to give him his change; he'd just turned on his heel and fled the store, back out into the anonymous shopping crowd. Now he was faced with needing to go through that again, risking humiliation at a sales counter by someone half his age.

He took a cotton swab from the box and dabbed it into the bottle. Perhaps he wouldn't have to go soon. Perhaps he could make this last a little while longer. He removed the gauze, and with a steady hand made the first pass over his bottom lip. The lipstick he had so painstakingly chosen earlier in the evening was erased as if it had never been. The waxy color from his top lip did not come off so easily, as when he had been concentrating on the chat he must have been pursing his lips, causing the mauve to bleed slightly along the left hand bow. Oliver discarded the swab, and turned on the hot water faucet full force. He went to take the face cloth from its spot on the towel rack, but opted instead to head to the linen closet to pull out a darker shade. There was no need to risk having someone at his laundromat questioning a mauve smear on a beige cloth.

He returned with a deep burgundy facecloth, and ran a fingertip under the flow of water. It was certainly hot enough. He dabbed the corner of the cloth under the water, and wrung it out with one hand. He daubed then scrubbed at his top lip when the color wasn't coming off as it should. He looked at himself in the mirror, his reflection appearing above the fog the blistering hot water from the sink had created. His beard growth did nothing to hide the red skin above his lip, and now he couldn't tell if he'd removed all the Mauve that had been there. He gave up with a sigh. He'd deal with whatever remnants there were in the morning. Heaven help him if he had to explain Mauve lipstick to Mama when he picked her up for church in the morning!

Oliver scooped up the box from the counter in one hand, and with the other swung both the cabinet doors under the sink wide open. Crouched on his haunches, he needed both hands gripping the box to maneuver it back into position. It was complete – it was done. As Oliver stood fully in front of his bathroom sink, he took a good, thorough look at himself in the mirror. He thought he looked tired, and because of the fatigue, he looked his age. He didn't like it. He didn't like the dark circles he saw under his eyes, that matched the ones he'd seen on his father for so many years. He didn't like the fine lines that etched the skin around his eyes. He most of all didn't like the jowl, the Garcia family jowl that was beginning to show on him. No questioning my parentage, Oliver thought as he turned from the mirror, turned off the bathroom and the bedroom overhead light, and crossed to his bed. He reached over and rechecked the stylish alarm clock next to his bedside lamp. Satisfied that he'd left himself enough time to get to his mother's prior to nine a.m., he turned out the lamp and curled himself around his pillow. The last thought that went through Oliver's mind as he pulled back the plush duvet, climbed into bed and turned out the bedside lamp, was one of mauve leather pumps, and church.

SEVEN

JULIA DELICATELY sipped her beer through a straw. She'd perched herself in the wings of the small stage that she'd spent so much time performing on in the past, watching the other queens perform. If this had been a year ago, you never would have caught her drinking alcohol during a show – it would have been lemon ice water all the way – but tonight Julia felt like celebrating. She hooked the heels of her shoes on the brace of the stool in order to keep her balance, as she swayed her body to the Aretha Franklin song 'Pink Cadillac' that was blaring from the speakers onstage. What a night! She had performed and it felt wonderful. There had been a slight hiccup with the opening song she'd chosen. Billy Bob Dick-wad, the DJ, had skipped the CD Julia had handed him earlier. Bastard. But she'd recovered well, and the remainder of the song, as well as the second, had gone smoothly, and was received with amazing applause.

Julia smiled to herself. Her last-minute email campaign had worked. The Wolves Den was packed to capacity tonight, and all her friends were accounted for. She could, at this point, head out into the audience and sit with her fans and friends, enjoying the remainder of the show as an audience member. But seeing as this was her first night back in a bit, she didn't want to piss off the other ladies any more than her return to the stage had already. She was content, that was all that mattered, she thought as she watched the other queens' performances going on through a gap in the wing curtains. Julia felt a hand rest on her shoulder. She lowered the beer bottle, allowing the straw to slip from between her lips, and looked over her left shoulder. Sophia was standing beside her, watching the performance as well, her eyes round orbs glazed with a

far away look. Julia didn't think Sophia knew that she was
mouthing along to the words, as she often did when the other
ladies were performing. Julia turned back to watch the rest of
the act, but brought one of her hands to rest on Sophia's where
it lay on her shoulder, and watched the remaining acts until it
was time for Sophia to close the show.

Sophia had been one of the first drag queens in New York City
to bring 'performance' into her shows. They weren't merely
karaoke songs performed by men masquerading in women's
clothing. They were full on classy theatrical performances.
And the audience ate it up. Sophia set the bar high for other
queens following in her footsteps, and found herself in demand
all over the city as bar owners knew that if Sophia LeRiche
was going to perform, bar sales would double. And she knew
it, so as her demand grew, so did her pay scale, and so did the
reverence due from the younger, less experienced queens.

Julian had met Sophia at his first audition. He had known
so little in those early days that he showed up in his male
street clothes, with pictures of himself in drag. He had had the
forethought to bring a tape with him of a selection of songs,
but that was all. A much younger, much lighter Sophia had
sat back in her seat and cringed as this gangly young man had
walked onto the stage.

Julian's stage fright had been palpable to everyone in the
room that day. He forgot some lyrics in the opening portion
of the song, and he had stood like a stick-in-the-mud, not
engaging the audience at all. His hand shook as he held the
microphone and even from where she sat, she could see the
sheen of perspiration across his forehead. Sophia felt a pang
of embarrassment for the young man. But once Julian closed
his eyes, and allowed himself to envision that he was standing
in his own bedroom, singing in front of his full-length mirror,

his whole demeanor had changed. Sophia had sat forward in her seat, enthralled at the transformation she saw in front of her. Julian became Celine. And Sophia knew that he would be her next pupil.

Julian had been scared stiff when Sophia had pulled him aside after that first audition. He was a relative newcomer to the cross-dressing world, and even newer to the performing side of things. But he knew of Sophia LaRiche. Everyone knew of Sophia. When Sophia had offered to take him under her wing and show him the ropes, to be an instructor of sorts, Julian, not being a stupid queen, accepted with gratitude. This was a once in a lifetime opportunity, and Julian was not going to allow it to slip away.

So he and Sophia began meeting twice a week, poring over magazines, trying hairstyles, make-up techniques, necessary padding, countlesshours of practice in the art of walking in high heels – nothing was beyond tutelage. It took months. Sophia took him shopping, explaining why the cut of a certain dress made his ass look big, why a certain style of collar made his own neck seem impossibly long and graceful. The correct hemline to accentuate his calves. The right fabrics to bring elegance onto the stage, how to carry a purse ... there were many things to learn. Julian soaked it all up like he did with all other information that came into his world – easily and completely – becoming more confident and aware of his allure each and every day.

One afternoon several months into training, Sophia took Julian out to lunch. She was dressed in her finest, although her makeup was subdued due to the time of day; Julian was in jeans and a tee shirt. Sophia had ordered a bottle of wine, and when the bottle was delivered to the table and two glasses poured, she raised her glass to Julian.

"Darling." she drawled.

Julian raised one eyebrow in response.

"Happy Graduation." she said, taking a small sip from her glass.

"Graduation?" squeaked Julian, almost choking on the sip he'd mirrored.

"Yes, my love, my pupil, mon petit chou. I have arranged for your performance premiere this coming Friday night. You are ready to take your first tentative steps towards womanhood."

Julian returned his glass to the table, afraid that if he were to hold it any longer his shaking hand would spill the ruby fluid over the linen tablecloth. "But Sophia, that's in just two days. I'm not ready – how can you possibly think I'm ready?"

Sophia covered Julian's quivering hand with her own, settling his nerves with her touch.

"I know because, my dear, I have been watching you. I have watched you when you think you are out on your own. I have watched you practice your routines. I've observed you in stores. You are as graceful as they come, Julian, with the stage presence of an angel. I know you are ready because I feel it in my gut. And my gut doesn't lie," she said, taking another sip of her wine.

Julian removed his hand from underneath Sophia's and placed both hands in his lap, hoping she wouldn't notice his fidgeting. The waiter approached and placed the entrees that had been ordered down in front of them both. Sophia delicately placed her napkin on her lap, and looked up to Julian with a quizzical glance when he did not do the same.

"Not hungry, ma chere?" Sophia asked, taking a delicate bite of her spinach salad.

"I've lost my appetite, Sophia," Julian said, his tone short. He pushed the full plate that was in front of him away.

"You'll need all the energy you can get, Julian. Please, eat. You'll feel better, I swear," she said quietly.

"I don't think I'll be eating much for the next couple of days. My stomach is in knots."

"That will pass, Julia. After all we've been through together, do you not trust me?"

"I trust you when it comes to many, many things, Sophia. This one – well, it's taking some time to process." Julian took a deep drink of wine, hoping the alcohol would squelch the butterflies that were flying through his belly.

"You have practiced. You have the outfit. You have the routine. You display amazing poise and grace for one so new to the field. What would make you feel more comfortable about this step that is so essential?"

Julian laughed to himself. "How does another couple of months' practice sound?"

Sophia rested her knife and fork on the edge of her plate, and stared Julian down with her eyes. Julian couldn't pull his gaze from hers.

"That, my dear, sounds like a coward talking. I didn't think I had so misjudged you." She sighed with resignation and picked back up her fork, stabbing at her salad.

"I'm no coward, Sophia," Julian didn't trust the strength that falsely showed in his voice. "I'm just scared. I could make quite the fool out of both of us. You know how brutal the others will be to me – it being my first time and all."

"You could, this is true, and they will be, this is also true. But you won't make a fool out of us. And I know you can handle the old queens who will try to break you. I've taught you how to prepare, and what to expect. There will be few surprises thrown your way – except, I have a feeling you will surprise yourself. I have faith." Sophia raised her glass to Julian, who resignedly raised his in return. The glass rang sharply as the rims met in a toast.

"Julian, from now on you will be only Julia to me. Julia NewMar. That is your true self, even if you can't quite see it yet. That is whom you will learn to embrace. Right now, this moment, you don't have faith in her, but I do. And I know what she is destined for – and it is great." Sophia paused; then raised her glass and said with simple conviction, "To Julia."

"To Julia." Julian said with some trepidation, and drank.

He sighed deeply, then gave in to his hunger. He'd perform, and do his damnedest to make Sophia proud. He picked up his fork and started on his salad.

∞

And so it had begun, Julia thought, as the performance she and Sophia had been watching came to a close. She swung her gaze again to the old queen standing next to her stool. Sophia looked back and smiled, obviously remembering as well.

"Well, ma chere, it looks like I'm up." Sophia said as the emcee announced 'the fantastical legend Sophia LaRiche' as the final performance of the night. The crowd went wild, almost drowning out Julia's next comment.

"Break a leg, Sophia." Julia said, as Sophia went over to the little mirror next to the stage and checked her makeup.

"At my age, it's more my hips that I'm worried about, lovely. But thank you." Sophie did a quick adjustment to her bosoms as she paused at the curtains to the stage. When her cue came over the speakers, she straightened her shoulders and made the sort of dramatic entrance that only Sophia LaRiche could.

Julia always enjoyed watching Sophia perform, and had tried on many occasions to emulate the style and talent that had kept Sophia steadily employed over the last 25 years. In trying to do so, she had developed her own style, and her own way of captivating and carrying an audience. A different sort of crowd adored Julia NewMar. She was the Sophia of the younger set.

When Sophia finally made her way backstage, Julia was waiting with a damp warm towel for her, just as Sophia preferred. Before Julia could reach out and hand it to her, she stopped short. The audience wasn't ready for the show to be over. It started with just a few patrons calling from the back of the bar, but the volume rose as more joined in, until the house was filled with chanting.

"Julia! Julia! Julia!" The shouts seemed to echo off the walls, receding and filling the theatre.

Julia was taken aback, and felt tears of acceptance fill her eyes. She held them at bay, not wanting to ruin her painstakingly applied makeup. She was distracted by the adoration as she handed Sophia her towel. Sophia, on the other hand, as soon as she heard the cheers, felt tired. She felt old. She took the towel that Julia offered, and with a crook of her head, indicated to Julia that she should go.

"They've missed you, ma chere. Go and perform. Perform for the both of us. Your public awaits." Sophia's tone was full of gaiety and light, but her eyes were flat and empty. Julia paused for a moment, unsure of how to ease what her mentor was experiencing. Because even Julia knew that this overwhelming response to her return was the passing of the proverbial tiara and sash. Sophia's time as the grande dame of New York City drag queens had come to an end.

Julia couldn't find words, and didn't know how she was going to be able to perform with the lump that seemed to be lodged in her throat. But as she turned from Sophia, and passed through the curtain, walking to the center of the apron, long stemmed red roses appeared from the audience, and Julia waved and blew kisses. And when the first refrains from her finale song came over the sound system, Julia forgot about Sophia, she forgot about the picnic, Christophe and Julian's broken heart, and any residual nerves. She had a public to entertain. And so Julia NewMar performed in front of her adoring public, and a new legend was born.

EIGHT

LUCINDA WOKE early on Sunday morning, and was restless. She'd never been one for lazing away a day in bed, but this morning she would have done anything to have a couple of extra hours of darkness so she could snooze. It was virtually impossible for Lucinda to sleep when there was an iota of sunshine flowing in through her bedroom curtains, so she found herself at 7:35 a.m. reluctantly ready to start her day.

She cautiously sniffed the air, and was rewarded with the aroma of fresh brewed coffee. At least she'd had the presence of mind to prep and set the automatic coffee maker when she got home from work yesterday evening. She swung her legs over the edge of the bed, and stood. Lucinda was comfortable with her own nudity, and didn't bother with a robe as she padded barefoot and bare bottomed into the kitchen.

It was her standard routine to fill her coffee mug and stand, leaning against the sink, taking her first tentative sips. She almost opted for the compact kitchen table, after the cool metal rimming the counter hit the skin in the small of her back, but reveled in the shock to her nerve endings. It seemed to help force clarity into her brain and chase the dopiness away.

She sipped her coffee and tried to make a plan for the day. Lucinda hated Sundays. She hated that stores around the city had restrictive hours. She hated that if she wanted to go out for a meal, there would undoubtedly be couples at surrounding tables who would throw pitying glances her way as she sat alone at a table for two. She had been trying to convince her boss to ignore New York State labor laws regarding overtime and allow her to work six days a week ... unsuccessfully. It wasn't a question of overtime and money; she was salaried, not a wage earner. For Lucinda it was a simple matter of doing her job. She had a project that could profit from extra work today. She resented being forced to place it on the back burner two days out of seven, when she'd worry at it during her down time regardless: look at the hours she'd put in last night! And if extra work brought personal accolades – even if it brought a better annual bonus – her efforts still helped the company.

Lucinda topped up her mug and brought it with her into the bathroom. She turned on the hot water faucet full force and sat on the closed lid of the toilet, waiting for the shower to heat up. How could she work without getting caught going into the office? She sipped her coffee and rolled some different options around in her head. She could phone into the IT person on call, and see if they could get her remote access to the databases. She could do some walking around Werner Street to see what her competitors were putting in their store windows. She could head back online to hit leather.com and AnneCole.com, sites she had skipped the previous evening. Or she could just bite the bullet and head into the office.

The last option won out. She'd hear about it through the rumor mill on Monday morning. No one, not even her boss, would confront her in person, but she had a way of overhearing exactly what she needed to know. Screw them all, Lucinda thought as she put down her half empty mug next to her lone toothbrush and stepped under the wide spray of the shower.

∞

Lucinda's confidence was brimming over as she crossed the empty foyer of her office building towards the security desk. She was dressed casually yet professionally, and the comfortable snakeskin pumps she wore made each step sound hollow. She signed in, showed her work badge to security and headed to the elevators. On the ride up to the 18th floor, Lucinda made a mental list of tasks to complete while she was there. First on her list was to head past IT and see who the unfortunate sod was who got stuck working the weekend shift. She hoped it was Willem. Willem von Helwan was recruited from the Germany office, and as he hadn't quite grasped the concept of small talk, he spoke a very frank English. He got along famously with Lucinda.

Secondly, Lucinda had to start breaking down some of the information the databases were holding. She'd already determined that a lowly intern could do all the grunt work, but she wanted to have everything set up so that when one of them pissed her off, and Lucinda could almost guarantee that this would happen within a few hours of her arriving at the office on Monday morning, she could head to that intern's desk and drop this doozie of a project on them. She smiled to herself, imagining the look on that poor nameless intern's mug when faced with hours and hours of tedium.

Lucinda rounded the final corner into the IT section of the office. She scanned left and right, not seeing a soul, then headed into the compact, cool room that held the computer servers for the office. She was pleasantly surprised to see Willem sitting there, feet propped up on a desk, reading the newspaper, humming to himself.

"Glad to see you're working hard, Willem. Are you having a good weekend?" Lucinda said with an uncharacteristic casual smile, as she leaned her shoulder into the doorjamb.

Willem shrugged noncommittally, as he looked at Lucinda over the thin wire rims of his glasses. He swung his legs to the ground and neatly folded the paper before standing and approaching her. "Sunday is Sunday is Sunday, no matter where in the world you live. It is a day for relaxation. No one should work."

"This is true, Willem," Lucinda agreed. "But why are you in here today? Is there some problem with the networks?" Lucinda tried not to let the nugget of panic his words created in her belly show in her tone. Having the networks down right now would put a quick kibosh on her schedule. And Lucinda MacHauley was all about keeping to schedule.

"No, no, no," he said and eased his lanky form past hers in the doorway, talking over his shoulder as she followed him down the hallway. Willem stopped at a small cubicle, devoid of any personal mementos that were evident at the others around the office. He typed quickly onto the keyboard, without sitting, then crossed to another. Again, he quickly entered some information, then turned back to where Lucinda watched.

"And you, Lucinda? I'm not surprised you are working Sundays, but what do you need from me? And so early too?"

"Well, I'm hoping that I can get remote access to a couple of the databases. Firstly, the one the outlets use to register clients. The second is the personal information for the clients who purchase over the Internet." Lucinda was silent as this request registered with the computer guru in front of her.

Willem was silent as he brought his fingers together and tented them, flexing them back and forth. "You know that information is confidential."

"I know, Willem, I know. But I'm working on a new project I'd like to pitch to Marketing on Wednesday. I can sit here for the next twelve hours and plug away using the internal system, but I'd much rather be comfortable at home, sitting on my couch. As you said yourself, Sundays are meant for relaxation."

"And if I were to arrange this for you, how long would you need access to his confidential information?"

Lucinda knew she had him. "Only until end of business on Monday. Then you can shut me out."

"The best I can do is give you access until five a.m. tomorrow morning. If it is any longer, we both run quite the risk."

"I'll take any time you can give me, Willem."

Willem sighed heavily and pulled a clean pad of paper from a desk drawer. He took one of the numerous pens from his shirt pocket and deftly shifted the lid from the tip to the end. "What is your IP address? I'll have to log you in as if your lap top were sitting here at the office."

"I have all the information right here," Lucinda said, opening her oversized purse and pulling free a cream colored piece of paper. "It's all the information I could gather off my lap top."

Willem took the paper she handed to him, and took a cursory glance over it.

"Okay. I'll have you hacked into the system within the hour. Will you have your cell phone on once you get home? I'll call you and walk you through the log-in process, it's going to be a bit more involved than you are used to." Willem's tone was stark; Lucinda could tell he was already hacking her into the system in his mind as they spoke.

"Of course. I should be there in thirty-five minutes."

"I'll call you no later than one hour from now."

Lucinda glanced down at her watch. Excellent. She tucked the purse straps back over her shoulder and took a step backwards.

"Willem?" Lucinda stopped, waiting until he had made eye contact with her. "Thank you. I knew you wouldn't let me down."

Willem turned back to the computer monitor behind him, grunted in acknowledgment or farewell, and started typing at a furious pace.

NINE

OLIVER LOOKED with bleary eyes at the alarm clock that was blaring at him. He groaned and rolled over, placing one plush pillow over his head. He didn't dare turn off the alarm, as that would be a sure-fire guarantee that he would fall back to sleep, completely missing his scheduled pick-up time with his mother. He threw the pillow to the end of the bed, and sat up.

Oliver Garcia was not a morning person. He sighed and swung his legs over the side of the bed. Routine was the only thing that got him through these first minutes waking, so Oliver didn't think, he just moved. He was zombie-like as he wandered into the bathroom and turned the shower on full force. Leaving the spray to heat up, he then headed into the kitchen to start coffee brewing. Oliver had prepped the automatic pot the night previous, so it was as simple as flipping a switch on the side of the machine to get the ambrosia started. That done, he automatically returned to the bathroom and stepped under the waiting spray.

When Oliver returned to the kitchen some minutes later, he felt slightly more human. The smell of the Tanzanian Peaberry coffee was one of his favorites, and he savored the tangy aroma as he poured his first full mug of the day.

Cup in hand, Oliver looked through his closet, trying to decide what to wear. He had business suits, casual suits, and so many ties that often it was hardly the simple decision he'd like it to be. It was Sunday, he was heading to church, and more likely than not, he'd be roped into dinner with his family. He sighed, and pulled out a Spring weight charcoal gray double breasted suit jacket, laying it on the bed. He returned to the closet, pulled out a light canary yellow button down-shirt, and hung that over the door of the closet. He then had the task of choosing a tie. He had structure to the order ties were placed on their rack. He knew the section he was looking for would accentuate the yellow shirt and grey suit jacket. He found one, a small gray diamond pattern on a dark gray background. Yes, he thought that would do nicely. He laid both the shirt and tie over the jacket, and returned for the third time to grab some slacks. This was the one decision that was easy for Oliver. He had light gray slacks that he liked to wear if he was going to be dining with Mama. They were slightly big for him, so he could eat to his heart's content without feeling uncomfortable in his clothing.

∞

Oliver jingled the ring of keys he carried as he waited for the elevator to arrive at his floor. He was running early – just the way he liked it. He would be able to take the scenic route from his condo in NoLita to his family home in Woodside, he decided, and twirled the keys once more around his fingers. The elevator chimed, the doors swung open, and Oliver stepped in.

He was thinking about ISYS and the trends she'd been talking about the night before when the elevator chimed again, having descended only about three stories. Oliver's head was bowed, and he was still absentmindedly swinging his keys to and fro. What did catch his eye were the set of women's legs and the fantastic pair of shoes that walked onto the elevator. Oliver couldn't help but stare. The calves were sculpted, like the owner spent a significant amount of her time spinning them around a stationary bicycle. The shoes were immaculate. They were some sort of reptilian skin, in a deep burgundy color. Oliver, although his head was still lowered, discretely allowed his gaze to follow the legs up to the short skirt that was swinging several blissful inches above the woman's knees. The skirt was the same burgundy color. Oliver cleared his throat, and tried to tear his gaze away from the shoes that were a mere couple of feet from his own. He was not successful. He could hear the muted chime as the elevator passed each floor, and he was silently hoping that there would be some mechanical breakdown so he would be able to continue his ogling for a few more minutes. His elevator companion shuffled her feet slightly, obviously anxious to be on her way. Oliver took in each slight give of the skin pumps, reveling in their obvious comfort. He made a note to himself that if he were ever to purchase another pair of shoes, he would make sure they were reptile and that they were that deep, rich shade of burgundy. They made his mouth water.

Oliver's eyes snapped up to the lit buttons above the door as the elevator sang out a double chime. Damn it. The ride had been far too short. What floor had the woman stepped onto the elevator, he asked himself? He wracked his brain, trying to remember, and in doing so, missed the woman leaving. He sighed heavily, and allowed the elevator to carry him down two more stories into the depths of the parking garage, his mind still distracted by the graceful instep of the woman who had stood beside him.

∞

By the time Oliver arrived at his Mama's house, his brain was clear again. He was a few minutes early, but that suited him well. Mama didn't move as well as she once had, so extra time to help her in and out of his spiffy little convertible was needed. She always whined about messing up her hair, when on a clear day Oliver opted to drive with the top down. But she always enjoyed herself immensely. She enjoyed the feel of speed that she could get no other way. Oliver was always willing to oblige.

Much to the amusement of his Mama, Oliver screeched to a halt in front of the church's wide front stairway. There were a few people mingling outside, all eager to soak up as much of the fine spring morning as possible, before heading in to sit through the service in the dark atmosphere of the church. Oliver hopped out and jogged around to help Mama from the car. She still had a smile plastered across her face as Oliver swung the passenger door open and reached in to her. She grabbed his hand, squeezing with a grip that belied her age, and between the two of them they were able to lever her massive girth from the compact car. She carried a cane, but Oliver knew it was more for show than for practical reasons. Mama could play up an old hip injury in the blink of an eye, and be limping like there was no tomorrow within an instant. Making sure Mama was settled on the sidewalk, Oliver hopped back in to the car and whipped around the parking lot looking for a free spot, then joined Mama in front of the church to escort her inside.

The Garcia family had been members of St Stephen's long before Oliver's birth. His parents had been married in this church, as had his grandparents, so it held a great deal of family history within its walls. The interior was dim. The stained-glass windows and Rose were small, and dark with grime and age. It smelled of muskiness and a hint of incense, which Oliver equated with an aura of sanctity. The floral display seemed out of place, as if it were left over from some forgotten wedding. It was, in truth, a typical urban church, getting by with less than adequate support from a declining congregation. Oliver hated the place.

Like so many his age, he was a secularized Catholic. He looked to his church to provide values and axioms to fit his active, secular life style. To some extent, he believed in Heaven and he believed in Hell. But he also believed his own relationship with God was a private affair. The God that Oliver believed in was understanding, and would forgive any transgressions a mere mortal had committed. But for some reason, none of that worked in Mama's church. Here, the God of the priest was more interested in punishment and repentance than atonement and absolution. It was as if the age and darkness and mustiness of the church had imbued the priest with an Old Testament fervor that left him feeling a sinner rather than simply a man whose weaknesses would be forgiven by a benevolent God.

Now, listening to the wheeze of his mother's breath beside him and the mechanical Homily of the priest, he sat on the hard pew out of pure obligation to his family. Family responsibilities weighed heavily on his shoulders. If his father were still alive, to be certain, Oliver would not be sharing this pew with Mama. He'd have been ... well he could be anywhere in the world. But the day the priest, the same one who had earlier walked up to the altar to start Mass, had called him to inform him of the construction accident that had taken his father's life, the ties that bound him to the Garcia way of life as a young man turned into constraints of steel. His fate was sealed that day, and Oliver accepted it as he had many of life's other twists – with a straightforward outlook. With help from the generous life insurance policy his father had left, Oliver was able to finish school without having to work part time. He'd been able to pay off the house his parents had re-mortgaged to ensure Rosella Maria was able to go to the finest of schools. But any youthful dreams Oliver may have indulged in died the instant he became 'the man' of the family.

Oliver had no desire for travel. He had everything he needed right here in the tri-state area. He really only had two indulgences once his father had passed. The first was the condo he had purchased. It had broken his mother's heart that he did not want to stay living at home. How would he manage for himself? He wasn't married, no girlfriend – who would cook and clean for him? These were constant questions that Mama had barraged him with in the months prior to his move. Mama, sensing that Oliver would not be swayed, asked of him only three things. The first was that Oliver hire a cleaning service, someone to appear while he was at work, and clean the place from top to bottom once a week. The second and third went together. Oliver was to accompany his Mama to church every week, and when he dropped her off at the end of the service, he would pack his trunk with food she had prepared and frozen for him. Oliver loved his Mama's cooking, and could tolerate the hour sitting on an unpadded pew or kneeling on an unforgiving kneeler, listening to the priest drone on and on if it would make her happy.

And the compromise worked. Oliver sacrificed his Sundays for his Mama. He allowed his mind to wander, tuning out the drone of the priest standing in front of them all. He knelt when he was supposed to, he sat when he was supposed to. He shared communion, and he celebrated the passion of his Saviour. But he was far away, in a shoe factory in Milan, a sensuous world of nylon, a slightly guilty dream world that mixed pain and joy. And while he knew Mama's priest would neither approve nor understand, he also knew he could live no other way.

TEN

JULIAN WOKE to a thunderous headache. Sighing with relief, he realized he had managed to make it home. He rolled over and glanced at the clock on his bedside table through partially opened eyes: Oh God, he'd got home only four hours ago. He groaned, threw an arm over his eyes to block out the sun that was streaming through his gauzy curtains, and rolled over. He reflected back on the night before, as his temples throbbed from dehydration and a hang-over.

Julia's encore had been like no other performance she'd ever given. The audience had been on their feet, clapping and singing along with her. There had been cat-calls and cheers – Julia was in her Eden. She'd come off stage breathless and happy, only to find that Sophia had gone, and only a few of the old-school performers stayed behind to congratulate her. That saddened her, but could not tarnish her high.

Julia had opted not to go back to the dressing room, as she normally would have done after a show. Instead, she went out and sat with her closest friends and fans. She allowed herself to be fawned over, her ego to be pumped up, and her veins to be infused with alcohol. It was a rare night indeed.

And now Julian was suffering the consequence of Julia's indulgence. He propped himself up on his elbows, testing the pain that echoed through his head. It was manageable, he thought, and glanced back over at the alarm clock. The desire to crawl back under the blankets and pull his pillows over his head was overwhelming, but Julian knew that there were other priorities this morning. He needed a gallon of water, a half dozen aspirin and a shower - preferably in that order.

He could hear rumblings downstairs that indicated that one of his parents was awake and starting the day. He knew that only one of them was up because there was no arguing echoing up the steep stair well. Julian sighed deeply and ran his hands over his weary face. Suddenly, the realization that the picnic was today came rushing back. And then his queasy stomach dropped even further. Christophe. Christophe would be there, with his new boyfriend.

Julian's shoulders slumped, and once again he had to resist the urge to hide. The slow steady throbbing in his temples finally motivated him out of bed. He wandered into the bathroom and turned on the faucet. As the water was cooling, he took a good look at his face. Julian looked like death warmed over. He grabbed a face cloth from the rack beside the sink and dunked it. After a good scrubbing to remove the remnants of last night's mascara from under his left eye, Julian looked at himself again. He didn't look much better. He rummaged under his sink and found the aspirin bottle. He tapped the remaining four pills into his shaky palm and filled up the glass that sat next to his toothbrush. He downed the pain relief quickly.

Julian turned on the shower full blast, and then closed the lid on the toilet. He unceremoniously plunked himself down on it, placing his head between his knees. How on earth was he going to make it through the day? How could he possibly cope with the pain of seeing Christophe with someone else? Julian felt the familiar pang of hurt race across his chest. He took a couple of deep cleansing breaths, then stood, the world and stars spinning around him. He stepped into the shower, hoping to wash away the cigarette smoke and stale alcohol smell that surrounded and clouded his brain like a fog.

∞

Julian was lying fully clothed on his unmade bed when there was a light tapping on his door. He didn't look over, but asked whomever it was to come in. His mother's face peeked around the edge of the door.

"Do you want breakfast this morning, Jules?" she asked quietly. "We still have quite a bit of preparations to take care of before we leave for the Park."

Even the thought of one of his mother's breakfasts, coupled with the reminder of the picnic, sent Julian's stomach roiling. He shook his head and swallowed the bile he could taste in his mouth.

"Are you ok? This isn't like you. You're awfully quiet."

Julian found a lump had replaced the bile in his throat and he wasn't able to answer his mother. Instead, he shook his head, his eyes filling with tears.

Margot was the epitome of a mother. She knew instinctively when her words were needed and when her mere presence was enough. She joined Julian on the bed, and pulled him up, resting his head on her shoulder. She rocked and swayed with her boy in her arms, and let him cry. Only when his sobs had slowed did Margot feel she should speak.

"What is going on, Julian? Was it your show last night? Did something go wrong? Was it a disappointment for you to be back on the stage?"

"No, Ma, that's not it." Julian sniffed, and sat back on his own.

"Then what on earth is the matter?"

"It's Christophe."

"Christophe? What has that dear boy done now?" Margot knew as soon as she uttered the words what Christophe had done. The mother in her wished she had the power, as she'd tear his heart out and feed it to him for breakfast. "Oh, my darling. When?"

Julian sniffled, and ran his hand and wrist under his nose. "A couple of months ago."

"But Julian, why on earth haven't you said something before now?"

"I just couldn't, Ma," Julian shook his head, "it's like I've failed again." Julian felt the tears reappear in his eyes, but he shook them off. "What makes me such a failure?"

"Ooooh, Julian." Margot pulled her only child back into a warm embrace, "You are not the problem here."

"But..." Julian started, but Margot spoke over him.

"No buts. You are fine. You know what you want. You might need to be a bit more choosy in your partners, but you are not a failure. Look at all you've accomplished! Look at the career you've set up for yourself – you're doing just fine."

"Julia doesn't have to worry about relationships. She's a stage act. It's me – me, Julian, that has the problem in that regard. I mean, you say be more choosy, but I've only ever had a half dozen relationships in my life. How much more choosy can I be?"

"Choosier than that damned Canadian!" she spat.

Julian threw his mother a look, her language and tone shocking him. Considering her acceptance of his lifestyle and the diverse people he counted as his friends, the vehemence towards his ex-lover caught him by surprise. It was mother love speaking, not reason, but he had to respond.

"The fact that he's Canadian has nothing to do with it mother. Neither does the fact he speaks French. He's just an asshole. Plain and simple. And he's broken my heart."

"What happened, Jules. Tell me. Maybe talking will help."

And so Julian spent the next three quarters of an hour talking to his mother, and his mother listened, ignoring the pressing need to get ready for the picnic, ignoring the yells from the lower floor from her husband, wondering why the eggs were burned. She was there for her son as she should be, and Julian appreciated it.

∞

The Rufailos made an odd trio as they crossed into Central Park and veered onto one of the many paved pathways into the centre of it. Julian had bags across each shoulder and a veritable vat of potato salad he needed both arms to carry. Margot had a knapsack on her back, and was laden with three plastic grocery bags teeming with vegetables. Isaak, also with a pack on his back, was certainly doing his bit by hefting the largest cooler he was able. Julian wanted to turn around and hail a cab from the closest street corner. He was still feeling the after-effects of his binge last night, and certainly didn't want to be hauling such a weight for a mile to the picnic site. They had only traveled the equivalent of a city block, and already his arms hurt and his legs felt like jelly. Despite the remaining chill in the late spring morning, he could feel the first rivulet of perspiration roll between his shoulder blades. Ugh. The last thing he needed was to be ill, sweaty and sore by the time he was faced with Christophe and beau. Julian turned to his parents, once again hoping to change their minds about the cab. He was faced with two resolute grimaces on their faces. Julian determined that if they could do the trek, he certainly wasn't going to be the wuss and bail. He plodded along beside them silently and sullenly.

∞

Lucinda was impatiently pacing a triangle between the windows in her living room, the kitchen table and her laptop on her stylish but bare desk when her phone rang. She answered quickly without looking at the call display.

"Lucy, I'm sor…" Hank started.

"Too little too late. Stop calling." she spat, disconnecting the call. With a few flicks of her well-manicured nails, she blocked Hank's phone number. Her house phone immediately started ringing. Irritated, she stomped over and turned off the ringer.

She glanced at her watch again, and contemplated phoning Willem. He knew when I'd be home, she thought, why hasn't he called? Was there a problem arranging the remote access? Once again, Lucinda paced the forty-seven steps it took to make a round trip – yes; she'd counted each one. On her next pass through the kitchen, Lucinda swung the door of the refrigerator open and removed a bottle of water. She continued to the laptop.

She all but leaped on her cell phone when it rang, agonizing minutes later. This time, she checked before answering.

"Hello? Willem?" she asked.

"It is done, Miss Lucinda. Now let me walk you through logging on." Willem's deep accented voice echoed back at her.

"Willem, what took you so long? I've been home over an hour."

"You are not the only one needing my services this Sunday. I had a router crash ... you don't want to know the details, but you are in the system. Now. Are you at your laptop?"

"Yes, I am." Lucinda pulled out the ergonomic chair from her desk and sat down, resting the cell phone deftly between her shoulder and ear.

"Alright then. This is the first thing to do..."

ELEVEN

OLIVER DECLINED the dinner invitation his mother extended to him every Sunday on their drive back to the house. His back had been sore since the night previous, and after spending all that time sitting on those wooden pews, he was in excruciating pain. All he could think of was getting home as quickly as he was able, taking medication, and calling Dr Warshinsk. Do not pass 'Go'; do not collect $200. His Mama offered to run him a bath and make a compress for his spasming muscles, but Oliver could only see home in his future. His shower, his heating pad, his drugs. Yes. Home was the only place for him.

Oliver was disappointed but not surprised to find himself alone in the long elevator ride up to his condo. He'd secretly been hoping that the mystery woman would appear again, and that he could ogle her footwear.

He couldn't contain the low groan that escaped his lips as he reached up to unlock his door. Fiery pain flashed across his kidneys, and he was more thankful than ever to be in his own place. He placed the bags full of frozen food on the floor just inside the foyer, dropped his keys on the small table next to the front door, and slid off his shoes without even untying the laces. He went straight to his closet and got undressed. He might be in pain every time he moved his arms, but his clothes wouldn't suffer. He hung them as meticulously as he always did. Only when he had laid the last sock on his laundry pile did Oliver head into the bathroom and try to soak out the soreness above the back of his hips.

∞

Oliver woke up, and rolled over. Amazing to him, he felt only the slightest twinge of remnant muscle spasms. He stretched tentatively, testing how well his muscle relaxants actually worked. He was pleasantly surprised. He sat up, adjusting the pillows behind his back. The clock next to his bed read just after 4 p.m. It was unusual for Oliver to feel so rested after a nap – even one that was medicinally induced.

It occurred to him that he had neglected to put any of the food from his mother into the freezer when he'd arrived home, so Oliver swung his legs out of bed, and without bothering to get dressed, went to take care of this domestic task, leaving out the meat loaf to thaw so he could nuke it for his supper. He opened his refrigerator and perused the contents. Deciding he'd run the risk of mixing alcohol with whatever muscle relaxant remained in his bloodstream, Oliver removed the opened bottle of Chardonnay, and poured himself a full glass.

He was slightly at odds as what to do. Usually, his Sunday afternoons and evenings were spent around the kitchen table with his Mama and sister, eating until he felt uncomfortably full. They would then retire to the sitting room, and play one of the numerous old musicals his mother adored so much. Oliver had, in fact, been named after the musical Mama had been listening to when she went into labor. He thought on many an occasion that it was fortunate Mama hadn't been to Kiss Me Kate, or Oklahoma at the time. Lord only knew what his name would have ended up being. Curly Garcia did not have a nice ring to it. Now, finding himself at home with extra time on his hands, he didn't know what to do to keep occupied. He could read, but dismissed that idea out of hand. His options were limited to television, or the world wide web. Oliver smiled to himself. He'd watch television until after supper, then treat himself to a little Manolo.

Oliver tucked his plate and utensils in the dishwasher next to the dishes from the past week. He didn't bother putting the machine on, knowing full well that his cleaning service would be in the following day. He was a tidy man by nature, but every weekend felt almost obligated to leave some sort of mess to justify the exorbitant amount of money he paid them.

He felt a slight pang of guilt when he curled up on the couch and flipped on the television. As Oliver was randomly channel surfing, he found an old version of Gilbert and Sullivan's "Pirates of Penzance" was playing on Bravo, and he knew for a fact that Rosella Maria and Mama would be sitting in front of the color television he'd bought for her a few Christmases ago, watching the same program.

∞

Julian was impressed by the turnout at the PFLAG Annual Spring picnic. He looked up from his plastic cup of lemonade and saw his mother in her full glory. She was surrounded by several other parents, and was telling quite an animated story. She caught Julian's eye, and raised her glass in acknowledgement. Everything had been running so smoothly. The volunteers who had donated their time to help dole out food had all arrived, and after the first wave of feeding, had taken a break to eat themselves. PFLAG parents peacocked around children who ran the gamut from the pierced teenagers who scared Julian a little, the butchy dykes with their crew cuts, baggy pants, and huge wallet chains, right to fully decked-out cross-dressing queens. Julian counted his blessings that his family was so supportive, and that they volunteered to help others going through the same struggle they had faced when he had first come out. Julian surveyed the crowd, and saw a familiar face. With a smile he walked over and pulled the short bespeckled woman into a huge bear hug.

"Crystal. You made it."

"Of course I did, you fool," she said, looking up at Julian and hitting him playfully on the shoulder. "After our party last night, I almost wasn't able to get out of bed, but I'm here now. Are there any bottles of water? I'm still humongously dehydrated."

"You and me both." Julian drained the last small amount of sweet liquid from his glass and wandered with his dearest of friends towards the food tables. He randomly lifted cooler lids until he found the one that contained dozens of bottled water. He picked one up, shook off the excess water and ice that had adhered itself to the plastic, and handed it to his friend, then pulled one out for himself. They both drank deeply.

"So, Jules, has 'Christophe the asshole' made an appearance yet?"

Julian's stomach dropped. "No, Crystal, not yet. He might not. The rumors might be true. He could, in fact, not even be in New York anymore."

"Bullshit. You know as well as I do that that bastard wouldn't give up a chance to rub your nose in it."

"Now, now, Crystal. Play nice. Claws don't become you. I know you never really liked him, but…"

Crystal interrupted, "No Jules, there you are wrong. I liked Christophe. A lot. I just didn't trust him as far as I could throw him. And that's saying something."

"Yeah, well, next time remind me to listen to your words of warning."

"Honey, you know I will," Crystal said, with a laugh in her voice. She hooked her arm through Julian's. "Come on, let's go scope for hotties." Julian laughed lightly, nodded, and walked off with his friend.

∞

Despite the sun going down relatively early, the picnic was wrapping up before any of the tiki-torches were needed to light the clean-up crew. Crystal had long since departed, having hooked up with a buxom blonde whose family was a new addition to PFLAG. Julian was helping his parents pack away what little remained of the pounds and pounds of food families had brought. Julian's father was in charge of stacking empty but dirty Tupperware containers into coolers, Julian was helping his mother scrape plates and collect plastic cups that seemed to litter the grass despite the numerous garbage pails sitting out. It was tedious work, but the Rufailo family was used to doing chores like this together, so the work was easy enough.

Julian laughed at a comment his mother made about one of the new parents. He laughed so hard he had to put down the plate he was scraping. And when he looked back towards his father, in hopes he had caught the story as well, that's when Julian saw him.

Christophe.

Christophe was leaning very casually against one of the ancient chestnut trees existing throughout Central Park. Julian felt his heart skip a beat and his breath catch in his throat. The laughter died quickly on his lips. Julian's mother followed Julian's gaze, curious as to what had cut off the laughing so abruptly. She put down the dish that she'd been holding so forcefully the crashing noise startled them all. Julian placed a calming hand on her arm to stop her from heading over to Christophe and beating him within a hairsbreadth of his life. Julian knew his mother, knew the look he saw in her eye.

"It's okay, Ma. I'll take care of this," he said quietly, and walked over to where Christophe leaned, digging his hands deep into his pockets.

Christophe flicked his head back quickly in greeting.

"What are you doing here?" Julian asked, unable to keep the defensive tone from his voice.

"My Aunt is a member of PFLAG, she got an invitation in the mail. I saw it, and knew I couldn't stay away. Mon cher, I wanted to see you."

Julian cringed at Christophe's use of Sophia's endearing French phrase.

"Why? It seems you wanted to communicate with everyone except me. What's changed now? Where is he?"

"So you heard rumors and believed them, eh?"

"What was I supposed to do, Chris?" Julian's tone bordered on desperate, "You wouldn't return my calls. Was I supposed to stalk you at work? The clubs?"

"Ah, Jule," Christophe crooned, bringing a hand up to tuck a wayward tendril that had escaped Julian's ponytail back behind his ear. Julian batted his hand away. "You are still angry then?"

"I won't play this game with you, Christophe. You made your choice. I don't think we have anything to say to one another."

"That is where you are wrong, mon amour, we have plenty left to say."

"Tell it to your boyfriend." Julian spat, then turned on his heel and headed back to help his parents, feeling sicker than ever.

TWELVE

OLIVER WOKE and grimaced. He was still curled on the couch, but an unknown ballet was playing on the television, not 'Pirates of Penzance'. He cursed the medication that still had such a grip on him. Actually, he had no one but himself to blame. He was the one that with full knowledge had indulged in several delightful glasses of wine while still being medicated. Oliver switched to the guide channel. It was after 11pm. I should go right to bed, Oliver thought as he stood and turned off the television. But because he had to cross in front of his computer on the way to his bedroom, the lure of Manolo caught him. He flipped on the computer and went to brush his teeth while his system booted up.

∞

It was with a satisfied sigh that Lucinda put her laptop to sleep. She still had hours of work to do, but even Lucinda MacHauley needed food. She stretched as she crossed into the kitchen, flipping on light switches as she went. She opened the refrigerator, and immediately wondered why she'd done that. She knew the contents, or lack thereof, like the back of her hand. If she were in a more resourceful mood, she'd make herself something; soup, a sandwich even. But she could feel her computer and the work remaining calling her back. She opened the drawer to the left of the sink, and removed a half dozen take-out menus. It was uncharacteristic that she couldn't decide right off the bat what she was in the mood for. She flipped the menus through her hands like playing cards, finally settling on Thai take-away. She replaced the remainder of the menus back in the drawer and walked back to get her cell phone from where it lay next to her computer.

She ignored the flashing light on her answering machine. The ordering was the easy part. Quick, simple, credit card given. The waiting? Well, Lucinda was not a patient person, so she flipped back open her laptop, determined to hammer out some more information and not listen to her messages, in the half an hour to forty five minute wait for her food to arrive.

∞

Julian dutifully dropped off empty dishes and containers in the kitchen of his family home.He didn't speak to his mother or father, just dumped things into the sink and turned on his heel and walked back outside, leaving his parents dumbfounded behind him. He didn't have a destination in mind when he started this walk, and he didn't particularly want to see anyone. He didn't want to talk. He needed to think. He walked for what seemed to be hours, solo, through his neighborhood in New York City. Anyone who saw him would know that Julian Rufailo had a lot on his mind.

Julian stopped dead in his tracks. He looked up at the brownstone in front of him. He knew where he was. He knew why he was there. This was exactly where he'd been heading for hours, and he'd arrived without consciously being aware of it. With leaden feet, Julian walked up the cement front stairs, and took a moment, the heavy brass knocker cold in his fist, before committing himself to this encounter.

The man who answered the door was portly, with hair so thin he looked bald in most light. His face, devoid of eyebrows, presented an average nose and a small mouth that had no upper lip to speak of. The eyes that met Julian's were as kind as any he had seen. Julian started to crumble as soon as their eyes met, and he was gathered into a warm embrace and ushered inside the door.

"Ma chere, what is troubling you so? This should be a day you spend reveling in the success you had last night. What has got you riled so?"

"Stephen. Or should I say, Sophia?"

Stephen inclined his head nonchalantly. "I can be Stephen the man and Sophia the queen. Call me what's comfortable, it matters not to me."

Julian nodded then continued, "I need to ask some advice. Man to man. Queen to queen. Can you help me with something of a completely personal nature? Something that isn't related to our mentor-student relationship?"

Stephen led Julian into the living room, and sat him down on one of the ornately overstuffed armchairs that flanked the couch.

"Jules, you know I would do anything I could to help in any way possible. Let me grab another cup," he said, indicating the tea service laid out on the table that was set for one, "and we can sit and talk until you feel better."

While Stephen was out in the kitchen, Julian took the opportunity to survey his surroundings. He had only been in Stephen's living room on one other occasion, and at the time, he had been so frightened of the man who was now crashing about his pantry, Julian had not fully taken in how Stephen and Sophia lived.

He crossed to the mantel that stood above a mock fireplace. What he found there gave him a little insight into the mentor he held so dear. There were a few generic childhood photos. If they were shots of Stephen, Julian couldn't tell. There were

the glamour shots of a much younger, much lighter Sophia
– Julian judged them to be from the late 60's. But there was
one photo that captivated him. It was a holiday photo, taken
on a beach – the location obviously tropical. A much lighter,
much younger Stephen was sprawled on a blanket next to a
lover. Julian only knew this was a lover because Mr. X was
looking at him with the most adoring eyes Julian had ever
seen captured on film. Both Stephen and this man were in
mid-laughter. It made Julian smile to look at it. He picked up
the picture and turned the light metal frame over. All that was
scrawled across the backing on the photo was 'June, 1968'.
No names, no locations.

Julian replaced the picture on the mantle, suddenly feeling
as if he were treading in territory not meant for his eyes.
He wandered to the tall, chockablock full bookshelf next to
the fireplace. He was seeing a side of Sophia's life that he
had never known existed. There were books on philosophy,
religion, art, psychology, erotica – the bookshelves held a key
to Sophia that, although it shouldn't, surprised Julian. The
Sophia he had known for the last decade was more than just
the determined Queen of The Wolves Den. She was more than
her exceptional talents in mothering new performers. She was
a multi-dimensional, multi-faceted man, whose interests were
as diverse as her song repertoire.

There was a light clearing of a throat from the wide French
doorway, and Julian spun around, guilt smearing his face in
being caught snooping.

"I'm, ah, I'm sorry... I was just looking... well, you have..."

Stephen waved off Julian's comments with his one free hand.
He crossed to the low table in front of the comfortable couch,
setting down the cup and biscuits he had been carrying.

"Don't concern yourself in the slightest Jules. My house is your house. You should know that by now."

Julian knew better than to comment. Instead, he took a seat next to Stephen on the couch, tucking one of his long legs under him, and took one of the plain digestive biscuits that were being offered.

"Milk or sugar with your tea?" Stephen asked, as if it were a normal occurrence to have Julian sitting down for an unannounced visit.

"Um, both I guess."

"Perfect, ma chere. Indulge in them all. Why limit yourself to a single flavor?"

Julian laughed lightly, and took the cup and saucer that Stephen handed to him.

Stephen sat back, crossed his legs, and for a moment, just looked inquisitively at the thin, worried young man who was nervously fidgeting with the little spoon on his saucer.

"Julian." Stephen said quietly.

There was no response.

"Julian?" He spoke louder this time, and startled Julian into returning his gaze, "What is going on in that head of yours? What question do you have to ask me, man to man?"

Julian's brows furrowed. He wasn't sure how to ask this question. He didn't want to offend. He didn't want to be seen as whining or childish.

Julian hesitated for just a moment more, collecting his thoughts. He took a deep breath and spoke.

"Stephen, how do you maintain the balance? The balance between Stephen and Sophia?"

Stephen's cup stopped part way to his lips, and then continued, as he took a dainty sip of brew. His cup rattled lightly against his saucer as he replaced it.

"Oh, Julian. You have raised one of the hardest questions a drag queen can answer - especially if the drag queen is one of your renown. I asked myself that same question many, many times over many, many years. It is not an easy one to answer, and my way will be different from yours."

"But you have managed it. I'm floundering here." Julian paused and shook his head, hoping to shake a little sense into the jumble of thoughts that were at present raging through his brain. "I have these dual personalities that are both wanting different things from my life, and I don't know how to reconcile them with each other and with myself."

Stephen placed his cup and saucer back on the table, sat back and stared Julian down.

"I managed it to the detriment of one of my personas, Julian. You flatter me by thinking I have it all worked out. Even at my grand old age, I do not. I have just come to terms with the choice that I made, and choose not to live in regret. Sophia is the one who is successful; Stephen is not. Sophia is the one that people recognize in the street. Stephen is the one that doesn't get a second glance from anyone. So Stephen is present in this house only. Sophia is seen in public."

This shocked Julian, and he didn't quite know to respond. He could see a glimmer of hurt revealed in his mentor's gaze and it made him slightly uncomfortable.

"And with relationships?"

Stephen sighed and stood, pacing slowly between the fireplace mantle and the French doors. He pulled the caftan he wore closer around his girth.

"Ah. So that is the crux of things isn't it? When you came in you thought this would be of a completely personal nature, nothing to do with our mentor to student relationship. In fact, ma chere, it is a lesson I should have made you aware of long ago. I was desperately hoping I wouldn't have to, as it would mean showing you my fallibility. And at the time, I needed you to think I was impervious to fault." He sighed again, and continued, "So, Julian, here is your final lesson, possibly the final words of advice that will cross from me to you. We all desire love. Julia, Sophia, Julian and Stephen. The love we desire doesn't always come our way. And sometimes when it does, we are too wrapped in our own life to let it in or to recognize it for the gem and rarity it truly is."

"I'd like to think that at the moment I'm more open than I ever have been. But still I can't get it right."

"That I empathize with completely," Stephen said, walking to the mantel. "I assume you saw this picture?" he asked, holding up the photo that had caught Julian's eye earlier.

"Uh, yeah. You look really happy."

Stephen crossed back to the couch and sat, handing the picture to Julian.

"That was the most blissful summer I can remember. I was in love, and I was loved in return. I thought I had found the man who would stick by me through thick and thin."

Julian's jaw dropped, "Can I ask what happened?"

Stephen nodded, but took a moment before answering.

"Sophia happened."

Julian was at a complete loss for words. "What do you mean?" he managed.

"That, dear boy, is Robert. Robert and I met at a Cervello's." He waved his hand dramatically again, "It was before your time, you wouldn't remember, but it was the place to see, be seen and to be picked up back in the day."

Stephen stood again and resumed his pacing, while Julian remained seated, not wanting to interrupt Stephen's train of thought.

"Yes, when I met Robert, I was convinced that I was invincible, that I could conquer and have anything and everything I needed. I didn't realize at that tender age what compromise was. I had no understanding of what the consequences would be. I just lived for the experience and dealt with what the fallout might be when and if it happened."

Stephen chuckled to himself, "I was so young then. What did I know?"

Stephen crossed back to the table, took a biscuit from the heaping plateful and continued to pace, whipping the cookie around as if it were a foppish handkerchief.

"At any rate, Robert and I were together and were so happy. We found a marvellous little apartment together in SoHo." He turned to Julian, "That was when SoHo was the place to live," he said pointedly, then continued. "I had just had my first performance, and Robert was there, first row, cheering me on with every song. He'd helped me put together the routine, the clothing and makeup, he actually surprised me by purchasing my first wig for me for that show. And it was an amazing show, Julian. Nothing like you see nowadays. It was true performance, none of this lip-synching. And I stole the show! I was asked back the following week, and it didn't take long before I was headlining the place."

"And I had fans, Jules. True fans. It was like a scene out of an old black and white movie. Flowers were delivered to the dressing room for me, and I had men, so many beautiful men who wanted me and would wait outside the back door for me to leave at the end of the evening. To say I wasn't tempted would be to lie, but I was truly content with Robert. He was the only person I wanted in my bed. I just wished he believed that."

"You see – Robert loved Stephen. He ended up abhorring Sophia and her hordes of adorers. He couldn't reconcile the two in his mind. And I, not being used to such flattery and attention by these other men, was swept away by it all, ignoring the destruction of my home when it was part of what I truly wanted. I wanted both.

And so you see, Jules, with the relationships you have, there is always some give and take. And it's going to be your decision who is going to take the main stage – Julia or Julian."

Julian was stunned, and more confused than ever. "But, Stephen, I think I can have both. I'm living both lives quite nicely, actually. I just had a bad break up is all. It has nothing to do with Julia."

Stephen sat, took the empty teacup from Julian and placed it on the table, taking both of his hands in a firm grip.

"If we are speaking truths here, then you must be true and honest to yourself too. You walked in here asking the question about balance. Somewhere deep inside you, you know there is a battle raging. I know what happened with Christophe. I heard the rumors and I know why you took a break from performing. But what I know that I think you don't yet is that Christophe was enamored with Julia. When you took a break, hoping to start that sedentary 'out of the spot light life' with him, he balked. He needed to have you be recognized and he needed to be recognized along with you. Can't you see?

"He felt better about himself when he was Julia NewMar's boyfriend. When you were just Julian Rufailo, he couldn't cope. You had the spotlight he so greatly craved, but he knew he didn't have the talent or half the passion for performing that you did. In my humble opinion, he wanted to be the strong man behind the famous queen. He wanted to be envied. So, ma chere, the question I pose to you is: who are you willing to sacrifice, queen or man? Because no matter how you try to maintain a balance between the two, there will be always be a sacrifice of one of them."

Stephen stood and gathered both cups and the saucer of biscuits. He made his way towards the doorway then turned back with one last comment. "It's getting late, Julian. Go home. Get a good night's sleep. Think long and hard about what we've spoken of tonight. I'm here if you need me, always, but next time? Please call first so I can receive you without being dressed in my nightie."

"Of course. I'm sorry." Julian stood and walked to his mentor. "Thank you Stephen. I love you."

"I love you too, ma chere. You know the way out." And Stephen turned and headed to the kitchen at the end of the brownstone. Julian, deep in thought, let himself out silently, and started the long walk home.

∞

The selection process wasn't as easy as Lucinda first suspected. She had thousands of names to go through. For her first search she put the sex as the criteria, narrowing down the list considerably. She was still shocked at the number of men who purchased through any of the Manolo Blahnik stores within New York City. She started to break down the list before her, then stopped. She should save this tedious job for an intern. It was difficult for Lucinda to stop midway through this phase of her project, but time was her enemy, so she printed the needed documents and moved on to the internet sales database.

She decided to take a different tack with this next search, hopefully cutting down the number of hours it would take to get a manageable amount of information. She entered shoe size as her criteria. It was startling how little the result numbers decreased. Had she messed up on her conversion calculations between women's and men's sizes? She didn't think so, but she knew where she could double check.

Lucinda logged onto the internet, and using her administrative password logged into Manolo Blahnik's website and then the message board. She glanced over the posters online, and found the one she was looking for. With a click of her mouse she made herself visible. She knew she was running a risk by doing so, as she didn't have time to sit and bitch with everyone tonight. This, she determined, would be a quick hit no matter how much people squalked. Lucinda didn't care if she pissed off some people in the process. Tonight she was all business.

She opened up a private chat room, and sent out a single invitation. She waited precious minutes before the chat was accepted.

> *DDDWide*: Yo, ISYS, what's shaking?
>
> *ISYS*: I only have a minute but I have a question I'm hoping you can answer.
>
> *DDDWide*: shoot
>
> *ISYS*: What size shoe does your husband wear?

There was a long pause, and Lucinda was sure that DDDWide was heading to the closet to check out a pair of her husband's trainers.

> *DDDWide*: he wears size 10 why
>
> *ISYS*: what size are your shoes?
>
> *DDDWide*: 9-9 ½. Whats this for ISYS
>
> *ISYS*: please.
>
> *ISYS*: i just need you to guess by putting his shoes next to yours what size he'd take if he were needing a woman's shoe
>
> *DDDWide*: ewkay...
>
> *DDDWide*: brb, gonna check

Lucinda sipped her water, tapping her fingers along the edge of her desk anxiously. Jesus Christ, DDD, she thought with irritation! How long do you need to make one lousy estimation?

> *DDDWide*: back

Lucinda was quick to her keyboard.

> *ISYS*: AND???
>
> *DDDWide*: well totally estimated, size 12 womens.
>
> *ISYS*: would you say hubby's feet are big?
>
> *DDDWide*: are you making a comment about the size of his... well... you no what they say...
>
> *ISYS*: no I am not.
>
> *ISYS*: what do you think...
>
> *DDDWide*: i'd say his feet are average - just like him

Lucinda grinned. This information was going to cut down her search tremendously.

> *ISYS*: Olivia, thank you. You have been really helpful.

ISYS signed off before DDDWide could respond.

Oliver sat back in his chair and inhaled deeply, slightly stunned. Well, that was certainly the oddest thing that had happened to him in a long time. First, it was odd that his shoe goddess would invite him into a private chat, and secondly, ISYS knew the alias he used when he registered at the Manolo site. Oliver laced his fingers and put them behind his head. Well well well, ISYS, who are you really? And what in blazes are you up to?

∞

Lucinda sat back in her chair and inhaled deeply. Well that certainly helped her momentary crisis. She knew that she would find DDDWide online at this time of night – well, she hadn't been positive, but she was certainly glad that her hunch had paid off. With a few quick keystrokes Lucinda entered her new criteria into the database search and went to get a fresh bottle of water while her computer chugged away.

Oliver scrolled back up through the chat he'd had with ISYS, and reread their banter in its entirety. He knew she was up to something. First there were the questions about men wearing women's shoes the other night, and now this? Did she work for Ann Cole? Was she trying to scoop ideas from Manolo Blahnik? Did she work for Manolo Blahnik? At that thought, Oliver's heart stopped cold. He tried to remember all the chats he'd been involved with, wondering if he had ever been less than polite when referring to a certain shoe style or design.

He dismissed this entire train of thought from his brain. Manolo Blahnik would NOT hire someone to masquerade on the internet. They would have no need. Any moderator worth their salt could stay invisible, watch the chats of unsuspecting posters, and report back to whomever needed the information. ISYS, if she did work for Manolo, didn't need to get involved. So, that left her working for the competition. You sly little minx, Oliver thought as he saved their chat onto his desktop. He then dropped it into his ISYS file, logged out of the website, and shut his computer down for the night.

THIRTEEN

MONDAY MORNING found Oliver up early, as was usual for his routine. His coffee maker perked away as he showered and chose his suit for the day. He had meetings to go to; he had clients to meet with. He was fully booked for the day. He had no clue how he was going to fit in an appointment with his chiropractor, Dr Warshinsk. He sighed and stretched, the ache still slightly apparent above his hip-bones, stretching across his kidneys. And as he leaned down to tie up his shoes, his back spasmed, crippling him. He groaned and sat on the bed, unsure of how he was going to get up again. Quite frankly, with the blistering pain that shot down his legs, and threatened to take his breath away, he didn't care if he ever got up again, just as long as this pain went away. He cursed getting old. He cursed the family genes that caused muscle complaints. His father, grandfather, mother and sister, all had some ailment or another to do with their muscles and joints.

For his father, it had been arthritis. And the arthritis that threatened his construction career and had made it so painful for him to wield a hammer or screwdriver had, in an odd way, propelled him into taking night classes so he could be a foreman. From foreman he had worked his way up to site manager and ultimately had branched out on his own, starting up his own small construction firm. He was happy to be master of his own business – the first in the Garcia family to do so since they emigrated to America three generations back.

Oliver's father had been killed in a freak construction accident. No one knew why he decided to head out to the site that day. No one knew why he'd not worn the hard hat, which was mandatory, and no one knew exactly what happened.

He was just found by one of the workers behind one of the many dumpsters that lay around the work site. The coroner and subsequently the death certificate had stated 'Natural Causes' as the cause of death, but Oliver had always thought differently. His father had been fit as a fiddle, had never had issues with a heart condition. Why would a massive coronary fell such an otherwise healthy man?

It was a question that plagued him. It plagued him as he stepped into his father's shoes to run Garcia Construction. It plagued him as he meticulously went through the books for the company, trying to get a handle on his father's unconventional accounting practices. It plagued him as he tried to console his desolate mother and sister. Finally, years after his father's death, Oliver resolved that he would never know, and in turn, decided to do what was evidenced by the accounting ledgers he'd been poring over. He decided to put the company in the black for the first time in four years.

He'd done remarkably well by his father's memory. He'd secured a couple of really big (by Garcia standards) contracts that by rights should have gone to other, more experienced companies. But folk in Montclair had loved Eduardo Garcia, and out of respect for the man, and respect for the son having to fill the shoes of his father, contracts continued to came his way. Oliver ended up building a reputation of his own, albeit based on the reputation of his father. He was known in the community as being hard on his employees, but no harder than he was on himself.

When the business had seen enough years making a profit, he had begun the 'Eduardo Garcia Foundation', helping under-privileged Hispanic youths learn a trade. It was with that foundation that Oliver spent most of his time and energy these days. Garcia Construction was thriving under site managers who had all started with the company at the bottom and had worked their way up. It was just as Oliver – and ultimately his father – would have wanted.

Oliver was jingling his keys nervously as he waited for the elevator. He hoped the woman he'd seen the day previous was a professional, and not someone who was brilliantly shod just for church. Not that a churchgoing woman was a bad thing, in fact it was an added bonus, but he hoped he'd meet her again as she was heading out to start her work day in some office downtown. He was hopeful when at the 7th floor, the elevator doors had opened, but there was no one waiting to get into the elevator car. So today he was disappointed. He rode the elevator down to the parking level on his own.

∞

Lucinda woke before her alarm, and had already showered and had her first cup of coffee before hard rock music started blaring from her stereo alarm clock. She was raring to go, and was anxious to get into the office. She felt an malicious flutter in the pit of her stomach thinking of the first intern who might piss her off, and the mountain of monotonous work she would pile on that hapless intern's sorry ass. She almost giggled to herself at the prospect. It had been a long time since she had been so jazzed about an idea for Manolo. She'd made excellent headway in her research the night before, and although she had used all but two hours of the time allotted by Willem, she was full of vim and vigor at the prospect of heading into work.

Her cell phone rang just as she was locking her front door. She picked it out of her purse and answered as she pressed the button to call the elevator to her floor.

"Lucinda speaking."

"Miss Lucinda?"

"Willem? To what do I owe this honor so early on a Monday morning?

"Just wanted you to be prepared. I think Stuartson found out about the hack."

Bloody hell, Lucinda thought. How on God's Green Earth did the head of Marketing know about a hack that wasn't even 24 hours old? Do I have a leak in my internet security at home?

"Well, shit. How do you think he found out?"

"I don't know for certain, but he's been sniffing about here since early this morning. I'm still trying to work out what alerted him."

"Well," Lucinda sighed, "Thanks for the warning. I'll take any flak that comes of this, Willem, don't you worry."

"I can handle my own flak, Miss Lucinda. Thank you all the same."

Lucinda's mind was racing trying to figure out what had happened. Stuartson was no fan of hers, despite her good work for the company. She didn't for a moment doubt he'd use her breach of database confidentiality against her if he could. Hell, she'd do the same to him: she could deal with that. Her bigger concern was whether he'd figured out why she'd accessed the database. She couldn't bear the thought of his stealing her idea.

"Look, Willem, I'll be in in less than an hour. Good luck until I get there."

"Luck. Right."

And Willem hung up, leaving Lucinda staring into her phone. She quickly grabbed her keys from where she'd dropped them in her short jacket pocket, and returned to her front door. She quickly unlocked each deadbolt and slipped into her apartment, hearing the distant ping of the elevator at her floor, the door opening and closing without her.

She didn't bother to take off her coat, nor did she remove the purse from her shoulder. She marched straight to her desk and flipped open the laptop that sat there. Her computer sang to life without her having hit the power button. The database loaded onto her screen. Lucinda cursed out loud and closed down the program. She then made sure that she shut down her computer instead of just putting it to sleep as she had inadvertently done the night before. Bloody hell. Was that how Stuartson had found out or did she have bigger issues at the office? She had been given until 5 a.m. to do her work at home. And even though she had finished her work before then, she had inadvertently allowed herself to remain logged in at 7:30 a.m. How could she be so neglectful after Willem had gone to such trouble and risk to help her? She berated herself as she retraced her steps to the elevator.

∞

She berated herself as she took the subway into Manhattan. She cursed herself as she rode the elevator to the 18th floor of her office building. She started to consider other security weaknesses as she strode towards her office. She was furious at the world as she walked down the hallway towards

Willem's cubicle. People stayed out of the way. When Lucinda MacHauley was 'in a mood' it only took one experience before you realized that you never approached her.

Unfortunately, the young, perky intern who happened to stop Lucinda in the corridor and ask a question hadn't read that memo yet.

"Excuse me? Can I ask you a question?" the girl asked sweetly, as Lucinda marched past her.

Lucinda stopped mid-stride, turned and walked back.

"I beg your pardon? Are you addressing me?" Lucinda asked, her voice thick with saccharine barely covering the caustic tone. "And who might you be?"

"Jasmine." the young thing chirped, not knowing that if you happened to ask Lucinda the wrong question at the wrong time and were smart enough to realize it, you lied about your name.

"Well, Jasmine, do you know who I am?"

Jasmine thought a moment, shifting her weight between the balls of her penny-loafered feet. "Um... You're Lucinda M., right?"

"That's right." Lucinda was proud that she was able to keep her tone somewhat in check. "Now Jasmine, do you see what time it is?"

Jasmine glanced across the walls and nodded when her gaze fell across the clock hanging there.

"Is it 8:30 yet?" Lucinda could feel the anger she'd directed towards herself honing in on a new target. And Jasmine, starting to clue in that she may have made a grave error in stopping Lucinda MacHauley that morning, was struggling to keep any semblance of a smile on her face. She shook her head in response to Lucinda's question, and Lucinda peppered her with another.

"Do you see I still have my jacket on?"

Jasmine felt her smile falter, and she nodded again.

"Do you see a mug of coffee in my hand?"

Jasmine had taken half a step backwards, and couldn't smile if her life depended on it, "Nn.. no." she managed, hugging the file folders she carried even closer to her chest.

"Then. No. Questions." Lucinda hissed through clenched teeth, and kept on walking down the hallway, leaving a shattered Jasmine in her wake. Lucinda smiled wickedly, and as she rounded the cubicle corner into Willem's area, she felt almost calm again.

Willem was waiting for her, but Lucinda started in before he could even open his mouth.

"Willem, I think it was me. I'm desperately sorry. I know how Stuartson may have found out about our little project yesterday. In error, I..."

Willem held up one hand, interrupting her, "I know. I traced the paths again. I know you left your computer on sleep and didn't log out of the program. I also think I have solved it. I rerouted the paths record, so it doesn't lead directly to you. I have no idea why he would check it, but I think we're out of the woods, as they say."

"Out of the woods? You haven't worked with Stuartson long, have you. He's like a dog with a bone; he won't let this be." Lucinda sighed, her brain moving a mile a minute.

"Ok, we'll let it be. Thank you for changing that routing thing... Thank you for doing what you do, Willem. And if Stuartson starts asking questions, send him to me. You don't need to be fielding his type of interrogation."

"What ever you say, Miss Lucinda." Willem let a little smile escape his lips.

Lucinda smiled in return. "Thanks again, Willem. You're the best."

"That's why they pay me the big paycheck." he flippantly replied.

"I think you mean 'the big bucks', Willem. 'The big bucks'," she said over her shoulder as she left his cubicle and headed to her office to start her day.

∞

Julian looked at his alarm clock, wondering where the last five hours had gone. Although he had been asleep, he hardly felt rested, and the dreams he'd had were strange in the extreme. He flopped back on his pillows trying to make sense of the images from his slumber that continued to play through his foggy brain. A waft of an image would pass by his closed eyes and would disappear as quickly as it had appeared. He sighed and rolled over, tucking his arm under his pillow. He nuzzled his head into his pillow and hit his alarm snooze button. Seven minutes' grace was all he could allow himself this morning. He felt the familiar pull of slumber, and let himself get dragged under again.

The blaring alarm clock woke him with a start after a too short reprieve. He sat up abruptly, and smacked his alarm off with one swipe. He rubbed his hands over his weary face. Damn. That seven minutes hadn't made him feel any better. He swung the duvet from across his hips and rose from bed, stumbling slightly on his way to the bathroom. He turned on the faucet, and rested both hands on either side, letting his weight carry through his fingertips. He looked at his reflection in the mirror. The shadow of a light beard adorned his fine cheeks and jaw line; his eyes, although still clouded with sleep, were a clear, vibrant green. The dark circles that appeared under his lashes were unavoidable, considering the last couple of days of his life. Julian splashed water over his face and began his morning routine.

His mother was standing at the stove as he walked into the kitchen. His father, already on his way to work, would have eaten earlier. Margot threw a look over her shoulder at her son.

"Eggs and bacon all right for you, Julian?" She asked, stirring the contents of the frying pan frantically.

Julian nodded, and got a well-used mug from the kitchen cabinet. He poured a mug full of dark perked coffee. He drank deeply of the black brew before he spoke, "That would be great Ma, thanks." He sat himself down at the table, and pulled out a section of the paper. He wasn't really interested in any of the news it held, but it was something to do in attempt to quiet his preoccupied mind.

His mother placed a plate of food and some utensils in front of Julian, then joined him across the table. She knew better than to pry, but she could tell her son was deep in thought, and troubled in some way. She would wait it out, as she had with other issues that had arisen over the years. So she ate, sat, and watched, hoping that her son would confide. He held the paper in front of himself, emulating his father and not realizing he did so. He was eating robotically, and his eyes never scanned the headlines or articles. In fact, Julian was so preoccupied he forgot he was eating, his fork stopped part way to his mouth, his mind a million miles away. He didn't notice that little bits of egg were dropping away, missing his plate entirely.

"Julian." His mother said, mindfully.

"Julian." She repeated, hoping to catch his attention.

"Wha-?" Julian snapped out of it, "Oh, sorry, Ma." He stood and dampened a cloth from the sink and wiped up the egg from the plastic table cloth. "I have a lot on my mind."

"I wouldn't have guessed." she said dryly, taking a sip of coffee and picking up a section of the paper for herself.

Julian returned to the table and grabbed his plate, dumping the remnants of his uneaten breakfast down the garburator. He placed his plate, knife and fork in the dishwasher and turned to his Mom. "Sorry. I'll, ah, grab a bite on my way to the store." He started backing out of the room, "Sorry -" he said again, and left, leaving his mother sitting helplessly alone, not knowing what to do for her son.

FOURTEEN

OLIVER WAS sitting at his desk at the Eduardo Garcia Foundation when his Rolex chimed the top of the hour. Nine a.m.. He flipped open his appointment book to remind himself of who he was meeting with, as for the life of him he couldn't recall. He had shoes on the brain in a very big way. Ever since the elevator door opened this morning on an empty floor, Oliver had thought about her. He knew that she was meant to get on that elevator, and he'd spent the better part of his drive into the office fantasizing about what their encounter would have been like.

The Monk's song 'Nice Legs Shame about Her Face' danced through his head. He shook it off; that had no place in his reverie. He supposed that she didn't have to be pretty, but in his fantasy she always was. Perhaps she too was Hispanic, or at least a fellow Catholic. He let himself ponder her potential looks for a moment, but it didn't last long. His mind's eye was always drawn lower, and lower, until he was looking at that graceful arch of her foot again. And she'd be wearing another stellar pair of heels. They'd either match or complement her outfit impeccably – of that he was certain. They would be smooth calf-skin leath... His intercom snapped to life.

"Oliver, the Cirveno twins are here to see you." Oliver cleared his throat and shook his head, trying to shake away the imagined scenarios.

"Send them in, Susan, please."

"Will do."

The intercom fell silent, and Oliver knew he only had about thirty seconds before the loudest, most obnoxious set of twins in all creation came ploughing through his office door. He glanced again at his day timer. Right. They wanted to donate part of their mother's estate to the foundation. Right. He needed to be charming. Damn. For a donation, even from the odious Cirveno sisters, he could 'do' charming.

Oliver stood just in time to greet the outspoken, loud, Long Island twins who walked in, looking exactly alike. Their hair was dyed the same 'too black to be natural', teased the same way, and they wore the same gaudy jewelry. They matched their clothing and accessories, from the banana clips that pulled their wiry hair from their over-made faces down to their matching black jelly shoes and coral painted toenails. Oliver cringed, and couldn't restrain a slight shiver that ran down his spine at the sight of those shoes. Jelly shoes!

"Ladies," he said, his voice a respectful low tone, "Welcome to our offices." He waved both Carmen and Celia Cirveno over to the two chairs that sat in front of his desk. Once both sisters had forced their overstuffed spandexed behinds into the uncomfortably small chairs, Oliver moved around to the front of his desk and propped himself in front of them. He dramatically clasped his hands over his heart, "May I offer you the Garcias' sincerest sympathies over the loss of your mother."

Carmen Cirveno held out one of her hands to Oliver. He dutifully held it in his own.

"Thank you, Oliver. I can call you by your given name, can't I?" Her voice was raspy, giving away the fact she had smoked Camels since she was 15 years old. The leathery face that peered up at Oliver had seen too many summers in Hawaii and was in desperate need of some heavy-duty moisturizer, and or some heavy-duty plastic surgery. Oliver made a mental note once again to call his buddy Julio and get the name of his plastic surgeon.

"Our mother knew your father. Did you know that?" Carmen was *so* Long Island, she pronounced 'father' as 'fawtha'. This was not a good thing, Oliver determined, shocking himself with the snobby tone of his thoughts.

"Really, I had no idea." he responded, trying to sound interested.

Carmen regaled him with tales of Eduardo Garcia and her mother Anne Marie, and their time in the old neighborhood. Oliver nodded politely throughout the tales, made appropriate 'I'm interested and listening' noises, but all the while his brain was logging him into the Manolo Blahnik website.

He managed to keep himself somewhat focused during talks of Anne Marie Cirveno's estate. He graciously accepted the check that was handed over by Celia, thinking uncharitably that he should call the bank and confirm the funds were available to be withdrawn.

"Now, ladies, when would you like to have the dedication ceremony? You know how many young men and women are going to get a start in life because of the generosity of your mother? From what you've," he glanced down at his watch and was shocked to see that over two hours had passed, "told me over the last couple of hours, your mother, God Rest Her Soul, worked hard her entire life. It seems fitting, doesn't it, that her legacy should be to help teach the next generation that same sort of work ethic?"

Celia daubed her eyes with her handkerchief, while Carmen nodded enthusiastically and held out her hand again to Oliver.

"I think that having a dedication ceremony next Thursday will do. Can we invite you over for supper afterward Oliver? That way we can get the business out of the way in the afternoon, and be able to catch up properly in the evening. You'll also be able to see the work your father did on our home. You know our father was one of your father's first clients when he started up on his own."

Oliver did in fact know that, and his memory of the twins suddenly came crystal clear. They had terrorized all the boys in the neighborhood, and rumor had it that one of them, (Oliver couldn't remember which one), had chased Robbie Torvello behind the butcher's and had kissed the bejeesus out of him. Robbie couldn't have been more than ten years old, and Oliver several years younger. They had scared Oliver on many occasions over the years with their over-bearing overt 'I want you and I'm going to have you'. Oliver felt a chill rise up his spine, and couldn't wait to have these two piranhas out of his office. He made a mental note to have an important business meeting pop up on Thursday afternoon. He'd be at the Foundation for the obligatory photos that would accompany a donation of this magnitude, but then he would unceremoniously bolt the premises.

"Well Celia, and Carmen," he nodded respectfully to each one in turn, "We'll be in touch with the final details." He ushered them both towards the door, adding "Make sure you leave all your information with Susan out front." Then he closed the door behind them both, not wanting the goodbyes to get drawn out.

He leaned his back heavily against the closed door, and let out a weary sigh. Crossing to his desk, he picked up his phone and buzzed his secretary.

"Susan? I'm going to be unavailable for calls or visitors for the next hour or so." He paused while Susan spoke, "Yes, I'll let you know when I'm free again. Thanks." He hung up the phone and let his weary bones settle in his chair. He shifted uncomfortably. His back still seemed to be holding a knot directly in between his hip-bones. He picked back up the phone and called Dr Warshinsk's office. The call was answered almost immediately.

"Drs Warshinsk and Myers, can I help you?"

"Yes, it's Oliver Garcia calling. I was hoping Dr Warshinsk could squeeze me in for an appointment this afternoon. I have an issue with my back that is screaming his name."

The receptionist laughed lightly. "I'm sorry Mr. Garcia, but Dr Warshinsk is out of the office at a conference all day today. Would you like to see Dr Myers, or can I book you an appointment with Dr. Warshinsk for tomorrow?"

Curses ran through Oliver's brain, and he shifted again in his seat.

"Let me just check my calendar here. Can you hang on a moment?"

"Of course."

Oliver flipped the page of his desk top calendar, and scanned the hastily written contents for the next day. He had appointments in the morning with new clients that couldn't be rescheduled, but he could futz with his afternoon schedule to accommodate an essential visit to the chiropractor.

"Thank you for waiting. Ah, does Dr Warshinsk have any free time in the afternoon tomorrow – say, after two o'clock?"

"Let's see..." Oliver could hear pages of the appointment book being flipped back and forth, "Certainly Mr Garcia, we'll see you at two p.m.?"

"Yes, fabulous, thank you."

"And Mr Garcia, have you been to see Dr Warshinsk before?"

"Yes, yes I have."

"Alright then, I'll get your contact information from your file. You're all set to come in tomorrow at two. Can I help you with anything else?"

"No, thank you. I'll see you tomorrow."

"Thanks for calling, have a nice day." The line went dead.

Oliver scribbled the appointment in his calendar. Good. That meant he only had one meeting to reschedule. But right now, he wouldn't worry about that. He had an hour to himself, and he was going to try to scour the image of coral painted toenails poking through twenty-year-old jelly shoes from his brain. Good God ... jelly shoes!

He turned on the monitor that sat on his desktop, and quickly typed the illicit words into the address bar. He felt uneasy doing this; he'd never before visited the Manolo site when at work. Nevertheless, he sat back with a slight wince and let the image of leather and sparkles take him out of reality for a bit.

FIFTEEN

LUCINDA SHUT the door to her office and leaned heavily against the cool buffed metal. An impromptu meeting had disrupted her otherwise perfectly scheduled day. She hadn't even had time to grab her first cup of coffee before the CEO's aide had found her on her way to the coffee room and had told her her presence was expected.

Lucinda was used to calling the shots when it came to her work, but she knew better than to slough off the CEO. She followed him into the conference room, and now, an hour later, finally found herself in her own office with mountains of work to catch up on. She placed her purse on the low chair next to her door, and slowly let her jacket slip from her shoulders.

Bloody hell. She still felt that knot between her shoulder blades. She grabbed the cell phone from her purse, and crossed to her desk, flipping open the small phone while she walked. She scrolled through the numbers automatically logged into her phone book, and let the cell dial Dr Warshinsk's office.

"Drs Warshinsk and Myers, can I help you?"

"Good morning, this is Lucinda MacHauley speaking. I'm scheduled to see Dr Warshinsk a week tomorrow, but seem to have tweaked my back. Does he have any free appointments this afternoon?"

The receptionist's tone stayed light. "I'm sorry, Ms MacHauley, but Dr Warshinsk is out of the office at a conference all day today – would you like to see Dr Myers or can I book you an appointment for another day?"

"What about tomorrow?" Lucinda's foot began tapping in irritation.

"I'm sorry, I just booked the last appointment for tomorrow with my last phone call. Would Wednesday do for you, or would you like to see Dr Myers?"

Dr Myers?? Not bloody likely, thought Lucinda! That maniac was sadistic – and without the playful benefits that came to Lucinda's mind. Time, she thought, for a different approach.

"Forgive me," Lucinda said sweetly, "I've been a somewhat regular client of Dr Warshinsk for some years, and I know I've introduced myself to you, but for the life of me, I can't remember your name."

"It's Laura," came the tentative reply over the phone.

"Laura! Of course. Well, Laura, I work at Manolo Blahnik, and we've got some fabulous shoes we want to get some feedback on. Nothing really formal, just real people wearing our footwear. You are familiar with our name, aren't you?"

"Oh my, yes. I adore his shoes."

"Well, Laura, I'm sure I could find a pair in your size and drop them around to you when I have my appointment with Dr. Warshinsk tomorrow. You could become part of our informal study, you see." Lucinda hoped that Laura would take the bait. Sitting with a burning lump between her shoulder blades wasn't doing much to improve her mood.

"Ms MacHauley? It looks like I've made an error, why don't you stop by the office around two p.m. tomorrow? I'm sure we can squeeze you in."

Lucinda smiled. "Laura, thank you. I can't tell you how much I appreciate your diligence on my behalf. I'll certainly be there, but please keep my appointment for next week open as well. Now, what size shoe do you wear?" she asked, jotting the particulars on the massive note pad she always had standing by on her next-to-bare desk top.

How stupid *are* these people, Lucinda wondered, shaking her head but thoroughly satisfied with her deal. She could get just about anything she wanted when she offered the right woman just about any pair of shoes. She flipped open her office laptop and started her day.

∞

Julian was still deep in thought as he placed the paper cup filled with steaming black coffee on the cement, and fumbled in his jacket pockets for the keys to open the store. This was usually such routine for him, he barely had to have his eyes open to get things up and running here, habit formed over the last three years of his employ. He dug out the keys and slid open the three massive deadbolts that secured the premises.

Julian picked back up his coffee and pushed the door open, flipping the closed sign around so that patrons could see the store was open. He placed his coffee on the counter and bee-lined to the back office to turn off the alarm. He flipped on light switches on his return trip, just as he usually did. Only today, something felt different. Usually when Julian, who had managed "Bras Boas and Belts" for the last year and a half, arrived at work, he was charged up. He loved helping the young clientele, mostly young drag queens themselves, find exactly the outfits they were looking for. Today his work place felt confining. He perched himself on the stool behind the counter and took a deep drink of coffee.

How was he going to help and be enthusiastic for his customers when he felt so jumbled inside? He couldn't figure out who he was, let alone see his way clear to help someone find out who they were, in or out of drag. And that kind of help was part of the reason the store was so popular; product was one thing, but support and direction was another. Julian had taken Sophia's spotlight on and off the stage. In his own way, he was a mentor to dozens of new drag queens in the city, even if he didn't quite see it that way.

He let his gaze wander throughout the store, and saw the displayed merchandise in a completely new light. He knew the inventory inside out and backwards, since he'd ordered most of it, but today – well, today even the brightest sequined gown looked garish. Even the pale ostrich feather boa he'd coveted when it had arrived held no appeal. He placed both elbows on the glass counter top and rested his forehead in his hands. Julian could barely find the energy to raise his head when the little bell above the front door chimed, announcing the first client of the day.

Julian raised his head, and tried to plaster a smile on his face. The person he was faced with could see right through the facade.

"Jesus H. Christ, Jules. Who killed your dog this morning? What's going on?" Crystal rounded the corner and pulled up a stool.

Julian could only shrug.

"Have you finished opening? Or are you gonna sit here like a bump on a log?" Crystal, even though she'd only worked in the store for the last six months, knew retail like nobody's business. She was competent and reliable, a retail manager's dream. The added fact she was Julian's best friend was a bonus.

"Have you counted the cash?" she asked, stepping off the stool, "Have you checked for deliveries?" She rounded to the front of the counter, "Jesus, Julian, have you done anything this morning but sit there on your ass and mope?"

Julian could still only shrug.

"Useless as a tit on a bull, I swear to God!" Crystal muttered as she headed to the back office to grab the float for the day.

He could only sigh and sit, staring off into space, wondering who he really was. If what Stephen had said was true, he would have to choose. He'd have to choose who he wanted to be. It seemed inconceivable that he couldn't keep both personas alive and well simultaneously. But what Stephen had said about Christophe was true; Julian could feel that in his gut. And Antoine? Antoine had been in love with Julia. He hadn't been able to deal with just Julian. And Rodger? Well, Rodger had been in love mostly with himself, but hadn't ever really been exposed to too much Julia, so the time he spent was with Julian.

Julian shook his head, more confused than ever. Who should he be true to: Julian the man or Julia the queen?

The bell above the front door rang again, and Roald, the newspaper delivery man strode in, his beefy arms swaying heavily under the load of two stacks of newspapers he held.

"Well, well, well. Julian. You certainly made a splash the other night! You're all over the trades. Welcome back." He plunked the two stacks of print on the counter and turned and left, leaving a dumbfounded Julian in his wake.

Julian was more than stunned. He was in the papers? He opened the small drawer underneath the till and rummaged through the miscellaneous pens, elastic bands, paper clips and spare till tape that were housed in there. He found an old pair of scissors and quickly snipped the tie that bound the bundles of newspapers together. He grabbed the top copy of the *Village Voice*, and quickly flipped to the Entertainment Section. And there it was, in bold print, splashed across the top of the first page. "Julia NewMar Is Back!"

Julian scanned through the article, barely reading the contents, and felt a familiar flutter in his chest. He put the paper down, picked up his cup of coffee, and started pacing around the short aisles of clothing. He wound his way to and fro, from the front of the store to the back, sipping and pacing past leather and taffeta. He made his way to the counter again, turned the paper around, and read the article thoroughly. He smiled. His smile grew wider than any he'd had on his face for the last six months.

He snatched the top paper from the second pile, this one a neighborhood rag but still a staple entertainment newspaper for any respectable gay man in the city. He found the review they offered easily, and read it from top to bottom, then read it again. Good Lord, he thought, they love me! His heart beat madly in his chest, and he knew in an instant what he needed to do. He could barely contain his excitement as he snapped the paper shut and went bolting towards the back office.

Crystal looked up, surprised at his hasty entrance.

"Crystal. Can you watch the shop for a couple of hours?"

"Sure." She sounded tentative, "Why? What's going on?"

"Nothing and everything." He was suddenly breathless with adrenaline. "I need to go do something, but I will be back. You can manage? What am I talking about, of course you can – with your eyes closed and one hand tied behind your back." He started backing out of the office, "I won't be more than a couple of hours. Thank you. Really. Thank you more than I can say." And he turned and raced out of the store.

∞

It had taken some doing, but Lucinda had found Jasmine in the bowels of the design department just after lunch. Jasmine had looked up, startled; Lucinda unceremoniously dropped seven file folders onto her already crammed desk.

"I have a very important job for you, Jasmine. I'm hoping you won't let me down."

Jasmine's eyes showed a hint of fear – smart girl, you learn quickly, thought Lucinda – but her voice didn't betray her. "I'll do my best, what would you like me to do with all these?" she asked, gesturing to the folders.

Lucinda pulled out a chair from the cubicle across from Jasmine's, sat, and proceeded to outline what she needed and the restrictive time line associated with it. Her explanation was both clear and concise; she could be a hard taskmaster, but she was a very good project director.

"Any questions?" Lucinda asked as she stood.

"Not right now, but if I do, when would be a good time to ask?"

Lucinda smiled down at the young intern.

"Any time after 8:30 a.m., as long as you see I have my coat off and a coffee in my hand. I'll check back with you before the end of the day." She turned back when she got to the edge of the partition, adding just a reminder of the whip, "Oh, and Jasmine – I hope you didn't have any plans for this evening. I have a feeling it's going to be a long night for you." And with that, Lucinda was gone.

As soon as Lucinda had cleared the doorway, Jasmine picked up the iPhone discreetly placed in her pocket and immediately started tweeting the latest on the Wicked Witch of the West (WWW for short).

∞

Lucinda tapped her elegantly shod toe impatiently as she waited for the elevator. She felt she was running out of time, and she wanted everything to be in tip-top shape for that upcoming Marketing meeting. She thrived under pressure, but it was never easy relying on the unknown qualities of interns. Lucinda lived by the motto "If you want it done right, do it yourself."

She stepped into the elevator, her mind full of possible 'Plan B's, just in case Jasmine did, in fact, fail. She did not acknowledge the other occupants. They, however, noticed Lucinda. Everyone noticed Lucinda. She carried such authority in her five-foot frame. She exuded personal power as others did perfume. When she exited the elevator at the mezzanine, she left in her wake two slack-jawed executives who'd travelled down with her wondering who she was and how they could finagle their way into an elevator car with her again. That was just her way.

Lucinda popped into the newsstand at the front doors of the building. She stood in front of the stacks for several minutes before she saw the papers she was searching for. She picked up a copy of *Village Voice* and an *East End Events*. From her own extra-curricular experiences, she knew these two papers were 'it' for getting alternative entertainment information. She paid exact change for them, tucked the papers under her arm, and headed back to the elevator. As she waited, from the corner of her eye she sensed that someone was staring at her, but by the time she had turned in that direction, he was gone. Damn Stuartson, she thought to herself, the bloody man has me paranoid. The weakness annoyed her.

When she arrived back in her office, she was shocked to find a bouquet of spring flowers, already unwrapped and in a vase, sitting in the middle of her desk. Lucinda knew immediately who they were from. She wasn't just unimpressed; she was livid. She kept work and pleasure as separate as humanly possible. Hank had no place in her work life, just as he no longer held a place in her personal life. Full stop.

She picked up the card that was delicately balanced between the stalks of pansies. She hesitated a moment, her hand hovering over the envelope. She was shocked to see her hand tremble. Lucinda MacHauley didn't tremble: she acted. Unceremoniously, vase and all, the blooms were dumped into the trash can next to her desk. She let out a shaky long breath. Done. Dealt with.

Gathering herself a bit, she crossed to close her door and sit back at her desk before she opened the first paper, opting for the *Village Voice*. She didn't have to look far. Julia was plastered over the first page of the Entertainment section. Lucinda read the article, then read it again more closely, going over it with a hi-liter pen. She shuffled the paper to one side of her desk and opened up the *East End Events*. Again, Julia was not hard to find.

This is going to be a piece of cake, thought Lucinda. If I can entice a lowly receptionist into giving me a non-existent chiropractor appointment by promising a pair of shoes, I can co-opt any queen into my plan with the same type of deal.

She snapped the paper closed, and sat back in her chair, elegant legs crossed, her brain running a mile a minute. A plan was taking shape, possibilities and contingencies racing through her mind. She was going to be a fierce presence at the Marketing meeting on Wednesday, maybe even getting Stuartson off her back once and for all. Lucinda could have laughed out loud, and actually would have if she could have guaranteed that no one walking outside her office would hear her. After all, she had a steely reputation to maintain. Instead, she giggled quietly to herself, and re-opened the papers to start taking notes.

SIXTEEN

OLIVER POPPED a couple more painkillers into his mouth and grimaced as he washed them down with a newly opened bottle of water. Mary, Bride and Jude, this pain had better be resolved soon, he thought and stretched gently in his seat. He mentally cursed Dr Warshinsk for heading to a conference today of all days. Oliver rolled his head on his shoulders and picked up his telephone.

"Susan? Is my one p.m. appointment here yet?" He listened for a moment to her negative response. "Alright. Show them in when they arrive please."

He hung up the phone and swiveled to face his monitor again, not wanting to waste these couple of minutes' grace. Manolo's Autumn line had been announced this weekend, and he was salivating over the new chocolate-coloured strappy stilettos rotating on the screen in front of him.

His mind wandered for a moment back to ISYS. She'd been percolating in the back of his brain all morning, and he was starting to put the pieces together. He looked forward to heading home to his own computer so he could open the file he'd created on her and the chats she'd been involved in, just to see if his gut feeling was correct.

He knew she wasn't the personality she put forth in those chats. He knew she had another agenda. But that in itself was neither unusual nor suspicious. Role-playing and deception were part of the joy of having an internet persona. He of all people knew that deception was ridiculously easy, as easy as it was addictive. He sighed, and moved himself further back in his chair, hoping to gain all the lumbar support his seat could offer, and moved his mouse so it was hovering over the chat room button. One click. One click was all it would take to get back into that world. He hastily moved his cursor and logged out of the Manolo Blahnik site. This was dangerous territory for him. He had never indulged before at the office. No one knew of his fetish – and what would they think if they found out? What would ISYS think? She hadn't seemed averse to the fact that some men enjoyed wearing women's shoes. At least it hadn't come across in her questions the other night – but if she did, would it show?

There was a light tap on his door, startling him out of his train of thought, and Susan opened it just far enough to poke her head around the corner.

"Oliver? They're here. Would you like me to show them right in?"

Oliver put his business face back on, thankful he hadn't been caught with the website blaring on his computer screen for the entire world to see. "Yes, of course." His voice was strong as he opened the bottom drawer of his desk and removed the file folders needed for these new clients.

∞

Julian was breathless as he took the front stairs up to his home two at a time. He unlocked the door, and sprinted up the steep staircase to his room, not bothering to wave or say hello to his mother, who was sitting in the living room reading quietly.

Suddenly everything had become crystal clear in Julian's mind. There was no question of who he needed to be. There would be no judgment from his family or from his friends. He understood now. It was perfectly clear – as if a God Light had shone down and highlighted three words on the page, causing them to hover and spin until he was forced to recognize and hear them ring true. "We. Love. Julia." They loved her as much as he did. In order to be fulfilled, Julian needed to live his life as Julia. Julia was just ... more than he could ever be, taking his best and making it better.

He winced slightly as he tugged the elastic band from his ponytail with too much force, and kicked off his trainers just inside his bedroom door. He went straight into the bathroom, and turned on the shower. He placed the elastic next to his toothbrush stand, and knelt before the cupboard under the sink.

He pulled out the hot rollers, placing them on the counter and plugging them in. He was determined that that spot would be their new home. He was done hiding the tools of his trade in a dark cabinet. He would be proud, and leave them out for one and all to see. Opening the other side of the cabinet, he pulled out his electric razor. That would be kept next to the rollers on the counter. The yin and yang of his personality. He giggled to himself. Yes, the yin and yang of his personality right next to the toilet. He laughed out loud and stripped his shirt off, dumping it on the bathmat. His other clothing followed, and he stepped into the shower. Julian hadn't been this happy in a very long, long time.

By the time he had stepped out of the shower, he was feeling more at peace with his decision than ever. He wrung any remaining water from his long hair, and after wrapping a towel around his sodden locks, he wrapped a second around his waist. He padded barefoot out to his closet. He opened his closet door wide, and as the light was still strong pouring in through his bedroom window, he had no need of the bare bulb that would illuminate the contents. He perused his wardrobe thoroughly.

Hmmm, he thought, I'm going to need to get more daywear. Hangers flipped through his expert fingers, and finally his hand rested on a navy blue wrap dress. It had been worn only once, at a Gay Pride Tea his mother had hosted the year previous. This is perfect, he thought, as he removed the hanger from the rod, and hung the dress on the doorframe. He knelt in front of the mountain of shoes that were strewn across the floor of his closet. He found the pair of matching low pumps easily enough. He placed them below the hanging dress, and went back into the bathroom to start his transformation.

∞

Hair coiffed, make-up applied, and appropriate padding in place, Julia inspected her reflection in the full-length mirror. She re-tied the sash on her wrap-around dress, and stood back. Yes. She looked put together. She felt put together. Julian and Julia were one and the same now. She could head back to the store and actually feel like helping customers. She could head out for drinks with Crystal after work and feel whole. Julia sent a cosmic thank you to Roald for dropping off the papers this morning and making the comments that would finally spur her into action. She flipped the long black trench coat across her arm, picked up the clutch purse she'd already filled with essentials, and sauntered downstairs.

If the appearance of Julia in the middle of the day surprised Margot, she certainly didn't show it outwardly.

"Julia! What are you doing home at this time of day? Is everything all right at the store?"

"Everything is fine now, Ma. Everything is just fine," Julia said, and continued out the front door.

∞

Lucinda put down her pen at long last, satisfied. Her idea was pure brilliance, if she did think so herself. She was itching to get the next phase of her plan underway. She flipped back a few pages on her pad of paper and tore off a single sheet, then headed off to find Jasmine.

Jasmine, it turned out, was in the office staff room, eating a bran muffin, sipping a mug of Earl Grey tea, and fiddling with her iPhone when Lucinda managed to track her down. When Lucinda barged into the room, Jasmine's hand, holding a delicate bite size piece of muffin, froze part way to her mouth. The other hand discretely slipped the phone into her handbag.

"Jasmine? What are you doing?"

"Having a coffee break, Lucinda. But rest assured, I've made great headway on the project you gave me."

"You'd be making better headway if you were actually working right now and not playing Scrabble or Tetris or whatever on your cell."

"Oh I don't like to..." Jasmine's throat seemed to close under the withering stare she received from her new boss. "Right." she muttered with a resigned sigh, and re-wrapped the remnants of her muffin, tucking it into the large purse she'd slung over the side of her chair. She stood, mug in hand, and followed Lucinda out of the room.

"Grab the files and meet me in my office." Lucinda all but barked at the cowering Jasmine who walked beside her. Jasmine fell away, heading to her cubicle while Lucinda, single sheet of fullscap paper still in her hand, went to clear an hour of time out of her schedule so they could talk.

When Jasmine finally joined Lucinda in her office, she was faced with icy silence from her superior, and the clicking of Lucinda's long manicured fingernails hammering out a staccato beat on the her desk. Jasmine sat, but had the good sense to keep her mouth shut.

Lucinda pulled the files Jasmine had placed on the edge of the desk towards her, flipping open the first one. She scanned the notes that Jasmine had made. The second sheet faced the same scrutiny. Lucinda's fingers flipped to the third, then shortly the fourth, fifth and sixth page. She looked hard at Jasmine, her tone incredulous.

"You've only finished A-C. What about the rest? You've had these files for hours."

Jasmine didn't know what to say. "Well, I've worked on it pretty much solidly since you gave me the project. I had a bit of my other work to do, and then lunch of course..."

Lucinda stopped her with an upturned palm and closed her eyes, trying to maintain some control.

"Perhaps," she said slowly, keeping her tone in check, "Perhaps I didn't emphasize enough the time constraints I'm under with this project, Jasmine. I need this done by end of business tomorrow. Tomorrow." Lucinda opened her eyes and looked at the quivering intern sitting across from her.

"Let's just take a different tack with this now shall we?" Lucinda said, sweetness oozing from each word as she slid the single sheet of paper she'd been carrying around with her across the desk to Jasmine. Lucinda felt a quiver of satisfaction to see the intern's fingers shake slightly as she picked up the page to read it.

"I want you to find this person. I've listed local bars where she performs. But I need to get in touch with her today. Today, Jasmine. That means you give finding her every second of your time until you meet her face-to-face and give her my business card, with the message you see written on that sheet. You don't stop for afternoon coffee, you don't stop at The Gap," Lucinda gestured about, like she was swatting at a fly, "or Payless Shoes, or where ever else you might buy your wardrobe. You find this woman and you give her this message. Today. Capiche?"

Jasmine nodded obediently, but Lucinda could see a question forming as Jasmine's brow furrowed.

"Don't worry about Mr Rivers. I'll talk to him about you being out of the office for the rest of the day. And before you ask, I'm serious about finding this woman, this Julia NewMar, by the end of the day. So, if you haven't had any luck by 5:30pm, call me here at the office. I'll have a back-up plan." She stood and crossed to the door, Jasmine moved to stand up, but was stopped by Lucinda's glare.

"Stay here for a minute and think of any questions you might have before you leave. I'll be right back after I talk with your boss."

Jasmine had never been in Lucinda's office before, and as she was too scared to formulate any meaningful questions before Lucinda's return, she spent the time looking around instead.

The office was bare. Not one personal picture on the wall. No framed degrees. No nothing. It was only when Jasmine shifted in her chair that she saw the top of a bouquet sitting in Lucinda's wastebasket. She leaned far forward, not wanting to be caught snooping should Lucinda return unexpectedly, but really, really curious. She reached over and quickly snatched the envelope partially hidden by leaves. Jasmine discretely tucked it in her lap, folding her hands overtop to hide it. She let out a quick breath wondering where her boldness came from. She concentrated on the sounds coming from the hallway. Nothing out of the ordinary. No barking Lucinda evident. Jasmine slipped the note free of it's envelope, quickly reading the contents.

Lucy,

You've obviously blocked my cell number, so being the persistent bastard that I am I got a new one. Please call me – we really do have to talk. I want to talk. Please. The new number is 315-744-9210. Please. Use it. Use me. I miss you.
–H

What the hell! Jasmine thought, the Wicked Witch of the West has a boyfriend? She's so uptight I would have thought her cooter was shut as tight as Fort Knox, security personnel and all!

Jasmine quickly snagged her phone and took a clear snapshot of the card before slipping her phone away in her purse and returning the note in its envelope back to the trash can.

Lucinda returned just as Jasmine's breath returned to normal after her subterfuge. She sat back in her chair and crossed her arms.

"Do you have any questions? Any at all before you go? Because now is the time to ask them. You can of course call me at any time if you are running into brick walls. But I have a feeling you are going to be resourceful on this one, Jasmine. Surprise me. Show me you can rise to the challenge."

Lucinda saw Jasmine square her shoulders and look over the paper once again.

"Find her, and give her the business card and message." Jasmine muttered under her breath.

"And what is your time frame for this, Jasmine?"

Finally, Jasmine raised her head and met Lucinda's gaze.

"Today."

"That's right," Lucinda smiled. "That's right. Now off you go."

∞

Christ on the cross, thought Oliver and he managed to stand and hobble across his office to grab a few more muscle relaxants, I am getting old. I must be, for this ache to be bothering me this much. Why in Hell won't it just work itself out? I don't have time for this shit.

He went back to his desk and gingerly sat down, pulling the keyboard closer to him so he could keep his back as straight as possible. He tried to refocus on the accounting ledger in front of him. But as the muscle relaxants started to take their toll, Oliver decided to give up his battle. He saved his work thus far, and turned off his computer. He stood slowly and made his way to where his coat was hanging behind his office door. It was harder than he expected to get the jacket up above his shoulders, but with a groan he managed it. He turned off the light in his office before swinging the door closed.

"Cancel all the rest of my appointments for the afternoon, Susan. I've got to head out now," Oliver said as he was passing his receptionist's station. Susan nodded, flipping open the calendar on her desk, and looked up to find her boss standing looking over her. She was glad he was heading home, as she could see he was in some discomfort.

"Your back giving you hell again? Would you like me to order a cab to meet you downstairs?"

"No, no. Thanks anyways. I'm just going to get a heating pad across my back for the next hour or so, and then I'll be better."

"It looks awfully sore. Do you have someone who can look at it?"

Oliver snapped his fingers, remembering. "Oh Susan, you're a gem for reminding me. I need to reschedule my 1:30 meeting tomorrow; I've already made a chiro appointment."

"Sure." she said, making a quick note.

"See you tomorrow, Susan. Thanks."

"Feel better." she said to his retreating form.

Oliver so wanted to be sitting at home. Unfortunately for his back, he had the pain in his neck to deal with first. God bless Family! he thought, only partly sardonically.

∞

When Rosella Maria emerged through the school doors at 3:25, she quickly ditched her gaggle of girlfriends with an eye-roll and a wave and headed across the street to her brother. Something was up. Oliver never came to her school – rarely talked to her for that matter, beyond politeness at Sunday dinners. She watched him as he straightened from where he was leaning on the side of his convertible. She watched him with guarded eyes as he straightened his suit jacket with one hand and reached for her schoolbag with the other. She relinquished it without question for no other reason than shock.

"Get in the car, Rosella."

"What are you doing here? Why aren't you at work?"

"We'll talk about that. Just get in the car."

"Is something wrong? You seem so tense."

He sighed just a bit theatrically. Why couldn't anything be easy with this one? "Seriously, Rosella, just get in the bloody car."

"You're scaring me, Oliver."

"I don't mean to," he said, wincing as he slung her bag into the back seat. "I just want you to get in."

She did as he said, and as she brought the seatbelt snugly across her school uniform, she tried to quell her nerves.

"Is something wrong with Mama? Did something happen?"

Oliver didn't look her way as he eased his car into the flow of traffic.

"No. Nothing's wrong. Not really."

Rosella Maria crossed her arms over her ample chest.

"What is it then? Why are you here? You've never picked me up before."

"You and I need to have a little heart-to-heart."

"You and… what? Why would we need to do that? We've hardly ..."

Oliver cut her off. "I know. But that's going to change. Starting now."

"Bossy much?" It was near impossible for her to keep the snark at bay. "Ohh ... that's right. Golden Boy is the boss." She rolled her eyes as she slid a little lower in her seat.

"Come on, Miracle Baby. Stop with the wounded child shit. You're seventeen, not seven," Oliver risked a glance at her, "and the pout you're sporting there is hardly a good look for you… ."

Her spine straightened slightly, and she forced the sneer from her lips, opting instead to stare him down. It didn't hurt that he was driving and could barely afford to spare passing glances her way. It helped her keep some control – never let the enemy see your fear and all that jazz.

Minutes passed in awkward silence. Oliver didn't care. He stole another quick look at his sister and couldn't help but smile to himself.

"Jesus, you look just like Mama with that frown on your face. Cut it out, it's creepy." He pulled into the underground parkade with the smoothness of long practice and slotted his baby into a numbered stall. He cut the engine, undid his seatbelt and released his door.

"You coming?" he asked as he slid gingerly out of the car. Rosella Maria, on autopilot, scrambled after him.

"Where are we?" she asked as the elevators slid shut.

"My place."

The shock of his simple answer caused Rosella Maria to blanche. No one in the family had been to Oliver's place before. 'Forbidden' was the term that sprung to mind. Shit. If Oliver was bringing her to his place, she must not be welcome at home anymore. She must have really, really blown it by sneaking out of the house last week. Or it could have been the skipping school incident. She sighed and looked to the ground, the corners of her mouth frowning as she raced through the catalogue of her many past transgressions.

Oliver let Rosella Maria stew for a while longer. He glanced up, watching the floors fly past. He shuffled slightly, looked down at the ground. He was appalled. Rosella Maria had on the requisite Catholic School uniform right down to the loafers. He shuddered. They were heinous.

The elevator doors opened and Rosella Maria silently followed him to his front door. He unlocked it quickly.

"Do you need any money for school? Your uniform okay?" he asked, as he ushered her in. She didn't answer, trying to figure out what he might be hinting at. She felt warier than ever.

"Nope. I'm good, thanks," she answered, standing just inside the jamb and leaning back against the closed door.

"Shoes," he said, pointing at hers as he bent down to his own laces, wincing. All school uniform shoes should be burned for terminal ugliness, he thought as he put his own away.

"I'm going to get changed. Grab yourself a drink – kitchen's through there – and I'll meet you in the living room. Oh, grab me a beer too."

"Beer?"

"Yes. Beer. Have one too if you'd like… ." He walked out down the hall to what was likely his bedroom.

Rosella Maria was shocked out of her inaction. She got two beers from the refrigerator, tossed the caps, and headed into the living room. She knew better than to snoop, opting instead to pick up and flip through an *Architecture Digest Monthly* from the coffee table while she perched on the couch.

Oliver joined her shortly, giving her the hairy eyeball when he pointedly moved her beer bottle from the bare table to the coaster it had been sitting next to. He sat across from her and snagged a coaster for his own drink, then leaned forward with a slight wince and held his bottle out towards her.

"Cheers."

"Cheers," she replied tentatively. She took a sip; it was what you did when someone offered a toast.

"Never play poker, Rosella. You'll lose." She blinked blankly at him.

"Your face. It shows everything, just like our parents. Must be in the genes."

"I have no clue what you're thinking, so that hypothesis must be wrong." She huffed and sat back. What the hell was going on? "Can you just spare me a morality speech and give me shit already? I know that's why I'm here. Mama must be so furious with me that she called you in to either be the heavy or to mediate." She sipped again. "You're not comfortable talking with me let alone being my disciplinarian, so you decided you needed liquid courage. Guilt made you offer one to me. Close?"

"Nope." Oliver couldn't help the smirk clinging to his lips, and tried to hide it by taking a swig of his own beer. He leaned forward, dangling his beer between his knees.

"I offered you a beer because, family or not, you're a guest in my home, and Mama's hand would come out of the sky and smack me upside the head if I didn't. I offered you a beer because I'd like to treat you like an adult – have an adult conversation with you. Beer is an adult's drink. Fair?"

Rosella Maria was taken aback, once more feeling uncomfortable. She didn't offer a reply.

"Don't worry, Rosella. This is between you and me. It's got nothing to do with Mama. Nothing you say will get back to her.

It'll be a secret between you and me." He stood awkwardly and walked to the window with measured steps.

"We've all got secrets, Rosella Maria."

Rosella's eyes never left her brother's form. She knew he wasn't comfortable having her here in his space; that was apparent with every tight word he spoke and each controlled movement his body made. Could she trust him? Did she have a choice? Oliver crossed back to her, but didn't dare sit. The depth of the chair would kill his back.

"So what is it Rosella Maria? School? Are you flunking something? Trouble with a teacher? Met a special guy? Or a girl?" Oliver smiled at his sister's wide eyes, knowing he'd shocked her with his frank talk.

"What? You think I'd judge you if you told me you were a lesbian? Tell Mama? Cast you out of the family?"

"You judging me wouldn't worry me as much as God judging. I'd go to Hell. If not for being a lesbian then for killing Mama, because the news would certainly stop her heart." She toyed with the rim of the bottle in her hands.

"It's not school either, my grades are good. My friends piss me off a lot of the time, but they're good too."

"So what's got you sneaking around, lying, and being a worry to our mother? It's got to be boys then."

Rosella sighed. She might as well get it out in the open. Who knows, if her brother didn't kill her, perhaps he would know what to do.

"A boy. One boy." There. It was said.

"What about this 'one boy'? Are you pregnant? Is he hitting you?"

"Oliver!"

"What?" He started pacing again. "We're adults, right? Having a serious adult conversation? This is how it goes with adults. I might ask questions you may not feel comfortable answering. But if you do, I should listen. I might not agree with what you say, but I owe it to you to listen."

She didn't respond, and the silence lingered. Oliver kept looking out the window, letting her stew. When he felt the time was ripe, he broke the silence.

"We're at the point where you get to talk and I get to listen, don't you think?"

She still hesitated. He could see her brain working a mile a minute, but still she stayed silent, watching him.

"We all have secrets, Rosella. Sometimes it really helps to share them. Sometimes as family, sure; but sometimes as adults. A burden shared is a burden halved and all that…"

She nodded, as much to herself as to him, and with a shaky breath Rosella Maria started talking.

∞

They were still talking as Oliver pulled up in front of his childhood home to drop Rosella Maria off. She had become quiet again. Talking in Oliver's apartment was one thing; being home was reality.

"You could just tell her."

"She would shit."

"That's what they make Depends for isn't it?" He glanced over at her, expecting to find her smiling. No such luck; her hands were tightly folded in her lap, her head bowed.

"Listen, little sister. This is *your* life. You are the one living it. Ultimately it's up to you to make sure you are happy. Sure, there are obligations. Good grades. Finishing school. Obeying your Mama. You're still a minor – but you won't be for long. Then it's truly up to you." She looked up at him, her eyes brimming with unshed tears.

"Mama wants you to be a housewife and raise babies? You know Mama: she wants grandchildren. So that shouldn't come as a surprise. If babies are in your future – near future, distant future – you can make her dream come true. Find someone you love and be the best wife possible.

"But you can be a business woman as well, or anything else you want to be. It doesn't have to be one or the other! If this boy William is around for the long haul, well Mama won't care if he's black, Muslim, or an artist. She won't care because she'll see he loves you and treats you well. She'll see you're happy. I think ultimately that's all she wants and all we can want for ourselves isn't it?

"In the meantime, we keep secrets. We all hide part of ourselves to make others happy. It works until hiding makes us too unhappy. Then a choice has to be made."

"What are *you* hiding, Oliver?"

He laughed softly to himself, seeing ISYS and sleek pumps, sensing cool nylon touching his body, having other hidden pleasures brought to mind.

"You have no idea." He straightened up, and tried to stretch his back out in the confined space of the convertible, still suffering from the pain. "But that's a conversation for another time. We'll do this again. At least I hope we will. I enjoyed it."

She smiled up at him, seeing him differently.

"I did too"

"Perhaps next time you'll bring that boy with you? I still have to be a big brother and make sure he's worthy of your Friday nights."

She released the door catch and eased herself out of the car.

"It's a date. Thank you, Oliver. Talking really did help."

With a quick wave, Oliver drove away from the curb. He was relieved to have met his obligation to his Mama. But Rosella Maria had come as a surprise to him; he had enjoyed talking things through with her, and promised himself he'd make time for her in his future. She needed some guidance. He could give her that, not just as an obligation to Mama, but as a responsibility he could bear as a big brother. His shoulders were broad enough to bear the extra weight. Except, he thought wryly as he felt a particularly nasty twinge, when his back was such a mess. With that thought, he headed for home.

SEVENTEEN

THIS TIME on the elevator ride up to his condo, Oliver hoped he wouldn't see the mystery woman and her shoes. He hoped she would still be working, and not be witness to his agony. He hoped that he wouldn't encounter anyone at all. He didn't want to feel obligated to exchange pleasantries. He just wanted ... well, he wanted ... he knew exactly who he wanted, and as the elevator chimed the arrival at his floor, he had a renewed energy about him.

When he dropped his keys on the small table next to his front door, Oliver sighed in relief. Home. This was where he wanted to be. The idea of taking a vacation, his first in six years, flitted through his mind, but didn't stay. There would be time for that, he thought. He'd leave the heat of the summer in New York City and escape out to the Cape.

He eased off his shoes and slowly walked into his kitchen. The counters were all wiped, and he opened the dishwasher just to be certain. It was empty, so yes indeed, the cleaners had been and gone while he was at work this morning. He sighed in relief. He opened the fridge door and removed the half-empty bottle of chardonnay that had been chilling in the door. He poured himself a full glass, and headed into the living room.

Oliver crossed the living room towards the leather chair that stood alone under the high window, picking up his portable telephone en route. He sat, placed his wine glass on the coaster that sat on the table to his left, and hit speed dial.

His call was picked up within three rings.

"Hello?" The voice was soft, with a touch of both the sultry and the exotic.

"Darling, it's me," Oliver crooned.

"Oliver! My goodness, it's been ages since I've heard from you. Are you well?"

Oliver took a quick sip of wine before speaking.

"I'll be even better if you can see your way visit me tonight."

There was a pause on the other end of the line, followed by a quiet "Urgent, or not urgent?" He didn't answer, leaving the decision in her hands.

"I understand," she said. "I'll clear my evening."

"You still know the code?"

"I remember."

"I'll see you then."

"Yes," she breathed, "and is it the same you'd like this visit?"

"Surprise me." he said, and rung off, tossing the phone onto the couch. He would enjoy the evening, secrets and all.

∞

Two hours into her quest, Jasmine was thankful she'd had the sense to wear her comfortable penny loafers today. She'd been walking for ages, and had yet to pull in any strong leads. Following the list Lucinda had given her to the letter, she'd already crossed off two clubs, neither of which had seen 'Julia' in months. She figured she'd stop at one more, and then damn Lucinda MacHauley; Jasmine was going to stop for a coffee.

Jasmine had never seen a drag show before, let alone met a real drag queen. She didn't know what to expect, and found the prospect a little daunting. She'd been in New York City for less than a year, after finishing her schooling in Virginia.

Like many others, she'd been turned onto Manolo Blahnik from watching 'Sex in the City', and had applied for a job with the company soon after moving. She was unsuccessful, though she'd interviewed well. She tried again six months later, and lost to a more experienced applicant. She was working retail jobs to keep food in her cupboard and pay her portion of the rent due at her shared apartment when the Manolo Blahnik office called to ask if she'd be interested in an Internship. The pay was crappy – maybe even less than she was making in retail. But it *was* with Manolo Blahnik. She didn't even hesitate. She had joined the firm just two months ago.

Her stomach grumbled, and Jasmine took out the remainder of the muffin she'd stuffed in her purse and started to nibble at it. She wasn't looking forward to heading to the next club. The Wolves Den sounded positively seedy to her, and if she hadn't wanted to work for Manolo Blahnik so badly and if the future opportunities weren't so attractive, she would have quit this morning after she'd been so berated by Lucinda. And if she hadn't quit then, she was tempted again after the reception she'd been given at the first club. But Jasmine was honest enough with herself to realize that at least a part of her was enjoying both the challenge of the unorthodox task Lucinda had assigned her and this forced opportunity to walk "on the wild side". She sighed to herself, and crossed another pedestrian-filled street.

She found the Wolves Den easily enough, and wasn't discouraged by the locked front doors as she had been at the first club she'd visited. She scoped the side of the building and saw the side entrance. She skirted the vagrant propped against the wall, and headed down to the door. She had her story down pat now, and felt her confidence rise as she knocked heavily on the steel door. She could hear the echo banging down the hallway inside.

She waited, but there was no answer, so she pounded again. This time she was rewarded by heavy footsteps approaching the door.

She stepped backwards as the door swung open. A burly man, his many tattoos glaring aggression at Jasmine, opened the door. He was clearly not accustomed to seeing a very female, very scared young women at his back door. "Whadda ya want." he barked.

"I, ah, I'm looking for Julia NewMar. I hear she's worked here recently? Um, I really need to get in touch with her."

"If you really needed to get in touch, why not just call her? Or are you not close?" If Jasmine felt he was mocking her, she would have been correct.

"No, she doesn't know me. But I have a business proposition for her. I saw the articles on her performance here, and I'd like to do some business. Do you know where I can find her?"

"Nope." He crossed his meaty arms, hoping to intimidate this annoying thing out of his doorway.

Jasmine pulled one of the business cards Lucinda had given her from her coat pocket. "If you happen to run into her before I track her down, could you please give her this card, and ask her to be in contact as soon as possible?"

Louis thought for a moment, obviously sizing Jasmine up, and weighing her story and the validity of the Manolo Blahnik business card. He wanted the best for Julia, and had been happy that she wanted to start performing again. If a tidbit of personal information given to this girl who looked like she was straight from a girl's boarding school could give Julia a boost, well, Louis would give it out.

"Her show here was a one time deal as far as I've been told. But she works at the Bras, Boas and Belts store over on 23rd. Try her there."

And he slammed the steel door in Jasmine's face.

Jasmine sighed and glanced at her watch. It was already 4:30 p.m. and she didn't want to have to be doing this after dark. She liked her job and the overtime pay would come in handy, but Good Lord, a job was only a job! She set off to head to Bras, Boas and Belts.

∞

Julia flipped the sign on the front door to 'Closed' and threw the deadbolt, flicking off the front light switch as she headed back towards the cash counter. Crystal was already ringing out the register, but Julia didn't need to see the totals. She knew they'd had a banner day. She'd helped, sold, and pumped up more queens today than she ever had. And she felt wonderful. It didn't go beyond Crystal's notice either.

"Well, Julia. This is more than a drag transformation you've gone through in one day. Do you want to grab a drink and tell me about it?"

"Oh, I'd love to, doll. Let's finish unpacking the orders first and then I'll take you out. I have some celebrating to do tonight."

"Well that's a deal I won't turn down!" Crystal said with a big smile, while rolling the cashiers tape into a tight coil. "Why don't you head into the back and start unpacking while I finish up the cash here."

∞

Lucinda flipped the last of the file folders closed. She had what she needed. After checking, cross-checking and rechecking her information, she had one hundred and fifteen solid leads on men who had purchased women's shoes through the Manolo Blahnik website over the last year alone. Conflate those numbers with the figures she'd gathered from the in-store databases, and she had the makings of a good business case. She was seriously going to kick some Marketing ass on Wednesday. But the case would be much stronger if Jasmine was able to track down Julia.

Lucinda glanced at her watch. It was almost 5 p.m. and still no word from the little intern. I will flay her alive if she comes back here with shopping bags, Lucinda thought casually, as she gingerly stretched out her back. The tightness was still apparent between her shoulder blades, but the piercing pain had receded, thank God. She could hold out until tomorrow afternoon and her appointment with Dr Warshinsk. Bloody hell, she thought, and grabbed her telephone.

"Nancy?" she asked, her tone a touch frantic, "It's Lucinda." She nodded impatiently to herself, wanting her co-worker to get past the obligatory telephone etiquette.

"I'm well, yes. Look. I need a favor, and I'm afraid it's last minute. I need a pair of discontinued size 7 ½ stilettos... Yes... That would do fine. Can I come down and pick those up now? Bad time? Okay, I'll grab them in the morning. Thanks Nancy." She hung up. Whew. Crisis averted. Laura at the doctor's office would be getting her shoes, and Lucinda would be getting her adjustment. It was the perfect barter.

∞

Spring in New York, and Jasmine was thankful for the extended daylight hours. She'd been walking for over half an hour, and she still hadn't been able to find this bloody store. She glanced down at her watch for the fifth time in as many minutes. Shit! She was late, and she knew that Lucinda would be starting to get nervous. She stopped at the next street corner and tried to orient herself. A deep voice rumbled behind her.

"Whatcha lookin' for, sweets?"

Jasmine spun around and was faced with the biggest blackest breasts she'd ever encountered. She looked down at the ground, and the legs were encased in the biggest, most purple pair of platform boots Jasmine had ever seen. Her gaze traveled up over the fishnets that poked over top of the boots, over the leather miniskirt that seemed impossibly short, back over the breasts to the most outlandishly made up face.

Jasmine took a moment before responding, her brain having trouble justifying the voice that came out of the person. Whoa, thought Jasmine. My first homosexual. Queen. Whatever.

She knew they were around New York. Hell, she realized she probably worked with some. She'd just never been so … up close and personal with one before. Not one in full drag. She swallowed deeply.

"I'm, ah, looking for Bras, um, Boas and Belts? My GPS says it should be right here, but I've been up and down both sides of the street and can't spot it."

"You're only one block off, in that direction. Stay on this side of the street." The queen pointed one of her dagger-like talons in the direction Jasmine had just walked. "It's only a small storefront, but the stock is amazing. I'd hurry though, they should be closing about now."

"Thank you, uh, Ma'am. I appreciate it." Jasmine sprinted back down the block, not wanting to miss her opportunity.

She'd missed them, she thought wearily, as she looked at the big 'Closed' sign in the door. She shielded her eyes, and tried to look through the front door pane. There was still someone inside. Jasmine knocked on the window, but got no response. She knocked again, harder this time, but only got a muffled, "We're closed!" yelled at her from the interior.

"I need to speak with Julia." Jasmine yelled back. "Julia!"

"Here, hon; let me deal with this. You've gotten yourself into a right mess," came the same deep voice behind her. The queen pushed Jasmine to the side and pounded both fists on the door frame, then bellowed, "Crystal, is that you? Open the door for Vonda. Come on now! Two minutes is all we need."

A shadowy figure approached the window and tentatively looked outside. Vonda waved her talons coquettishly. They both heard the deadbolts being unlatched, and the door was opened.

"Vonda, good Christ! We're closed; you can see that. What the fuck do you want?"

"I want you to talk to this young thing. She's been walking around in this neighborhood for ages looking for you and Julia. Give her a minute of your time." Crystal started to protest, but Vonda shut her down. "Two minutes, Crystal – be charitable."

"Ah shit!" was the response, as the door opened and Crystal, obviously less than thrilled when she turned and scoped Jasmine from head to toe, offered only a brusque "What are *you* after?"

"I need to talk to Julia. Is she working today?"

"She might be, why do you need her?"

"It's a business thing," Jasmine gushed. She felt incredibly nervous, being flanked by the biggest, blackest drag queen in New York City, and being stared down by the butchiest dyke she'd ever faced. She felt acutely uncomfortable, and quite frankly after the day she'd had today, Jasmine just wanted this over and to be able to go home to her safe apartment and not too psychotic roommate.

"Look, I don't know exactly what's going on. I work for Manolo Blahnik and one of our R&D reps heard of, or read about, Julia NewMar and wants to speak with her. I don't know much else, I'm only an intern there, but I have a message and card." Jasmine once again pulled a business card from her pocket, which Crystal snatched and inspected thoroughly.

"Stay here." Crystal said, and shut the door. Which left an awkward, embarrassed Jasmine with a far too comfortable Vonda.

"Vonda? Thanks for your help," Jasmine managed.

"Hon, no problem. Sometimes you gotta pull out the big guns to get things done 'round here."

"So you're considered the 'big gun' of the neighborhood?" Jasmine asked, hoping that Crystal would return soon. Small talk, especially with a big black cross-dresser, was hardly her specialty.

"Hon, there is no bigger gun on the block, if you know what I mean." Vonda's hand cupped her crotch momentarily, chuckled deep in here throat, and went back to inspecting her abnormally long nails.

"Ah, right... Well... good for you." Jasmine tried to cover her unease by staring back into the window of the store, and saw a figure approaching. The front door of the store opened, and a slight, extremely feminine face peered out.

"Are you looking for me?" asked the gentle male voice.

"Are you Julia?" Jasmine asked, her eyes wide.

"I am. And are you Lucinda?"

Jasmine couldn't restrain a guffaw that echoed through the evening.

"Uh, no. No! I'm just an intern – I report to Lucinda on this project – at Manolo. But Lucinda told me to find you. Today.

She'd like to set up a meeting. Did that other woman give you her business card?"

"No, as a matter of fact, she didn't." The slight laugh in those words made Jasmine smile as well. "I think Crystal may have kept it for her own reasons. Do you have another you could spare?"

Jasmine reached into her pocket and pulled out another card, and placed it in the hand that snaked around the edge of the door frame. Julia inspected the card, and then swung the door open wide.

"You might as well come in."

Jasmine was let into the small store, but Julia held her hand across the threshold preventing Vonda's entrance.

"Just the girl, Vonda."

"But now you got me all curious. Manolo meaning Blahnik Manolo? As in the shoes? Those shoes are gorgeous! Not for sausages like these, maybe," she pointed one toe forward and gazed down to it, "but a girl can dream."

"Thanks for getting Crystal's attention so we could open up, but I think this is more of a private matter. Good night, Vonda." Julia said firmly.

"But I won't even talk, I'll just listen in. C'mon, Julia. Give me a little bit of scoop. The rumor mill has been so slow over the last couple of months, since you and Christophe... I mean, since you decided to stop perf... ." Vonda let out a defeated sigh when she saw the determined look in Julia's eyes.

"Fine. You don't let me come in, I'm staying right outside this door. I can still hear, ya know. I have ears that can pick up plenty through these flimsy glass windows."

"You can stand wherever you want, Von, you're just not coming in. Private is private."

Julia shut the door and threw the deadbolt, but both she and Jasmine could see the black face just beyond the beveled glass of the door window.

Julia indicated that Jasmine should follow her to the back of the store. Jasmine was hoping there weren't too many questions. She had far too few answers.

Julia stepped into the cramped back office, where Crystal was waiting. Jasmine followed. Julia crossed her arms and turned to Jasmine almost aggressively. "So what sort of game are you playing at?"

"Game? Playing?" Jasmine was taken aback, not expecting this reception at all, especially after what had transpired at the front door. "I'm not playing at all; I'm just doing what I'm told. With Lucinda, there's no room for games."

"Why would a rep from Manolo Blahnik be looking for me? Me! Why would a rep from Manolo Blahnik send out some intern to track me down? Did Christophe put you up to this?"

"Christophe?" Jasmine choked, "Who's he?" Suddenly nervous, she took half a step backwards so she was a little closer to the door.

"Look. I'm just the messenger. I was told to find you and give you the card and the message. I have done both. I don't know what Lucinda has planned. But I've done my job. Just call her and find out, okay? I'd better be leaving." Jasmine turned to head towards the front of the store. A hand on her shoulder stopped her.

"Oh no you don't. You're staying right here while I make this phone call. Crystal?"

"Right behind you."

"Watch this one, please."

There was no way Jasmine was doing battle with the woman standing in front of her, looking like she could bite the head off nails if given the opportunity, so she crossed her arms, mirroring Crystal, and waited.

∞

Lucinda sat tapping her toes anxiously. She could hear people in the corridor saying their good-nights. She wasn't going anywhere until that phone rang. And if it was 8:30 in the morning before Lucinda left her office, there was certainly going to be hell to pay when she saw Jasmine next. She logged onto her computer, and was just heading into the Manolo site with her administrative password when her phone rang. She picked it up immediately.

"Lucinda MacHauley."

"Hello. This is Julia NewMar. I believe you are looking for me?"

Lucinda let out a sigh of relief. Thank you Jasmine, she thought. "Ms NewMar. Thank you for calling so promptly."

"I almost didn't. I thought this was some sort of prank, but I got patched through Manolo's switchboard, and that would be hard to pull off if this were a joke."

"Ms NewMar, this is no joke." Lucinda said, sitting back in her chair and swinging her elegant legs onto the desktop. She winced slightly and placed her feet back on the ground. "I need your help and have a bit of a business proposition for you."

"I'm listening."

The hint of aggression, the touch of scepticism in Julia's voice caught Lucinda by surprise, adding a complexity she hadn't anticipated. This might not work over the phone, she thought, knowing she could be more persuasive in person, turning on a personal charm that could never be conveyed over a telephone.

"Why don't you let me know where I can meet you, I'll buy you a drink and we'll talk."

"I don't think so," came the hesitant reply. That wasn't the response Lucinda was expecting.

"It will be worth your while, I swear. This is no joke. I know you frequent the Manolo Blahnik website and chat rooms. I know you purchased two pairs of pumps in a size 12, the first in December three years ago and the second in July last year. I know the design and color you ordered them in. I have all your billing information here. Except your phone number. That has been absent on all records we have for you.

"You have visited the message boards from time to time, using JuliaNewMar as your handle, but obviously haven't been on in the last few days or you would have seen the instant messages I've been leaving for you."

"So you hacked into the database" Julia responded, "which I find disturbing, to be honest, but no big deal. What could possibly be so important you have to send some minion into SoHo to track me down?"

Lucinda sighed, "Are you sure you won't meet with me, Julia? Just one drink? It will be mutually beneficial. I'll bring a pair of pumps in your size with me as a token of my appreciation for your time."

"How do I know that you'll show? Or who might show up with you. How do I really know this isn't some sort of elaborate joke? And why do you assume you can bribe me, particularly with a pair of last season's oversized discards?"

"Right now, Julia, I guess you don't. But bring Jasmine with you. She might want to refuse, but I'm sure you can convince her to join us just by telling her I want her there. She'll understand."

Lucinda went into her most persuasive tone. "You name the bar and the time Julia, and I'll be there."

Julia thought for a moment. Hell. This Lucinda woman was willing to spring for drinks and would bring shoes? Julia threw Julian's over-cautious nature to the wind and accepted.

"Meet me at the Rovers. It's at..."

"I know where it is," Lucinda said, smiling like a Cheshire cat, adding pointedly, "and I'll bring you a new pair of pumps – not discounted but this season's – as I said I would." Greedy bitch, she muttered to herself as she hung up the phone. At this rate, I'll have used up all my clout with Nancy by the end of the season. Julia had better be worth it!

∞

It was several minutes before a thoughtful Julia made her way back to Crystal and Jasmine.

"Come on ladies, we're gonna meet somebody for a drink." Julia shoved Crystal's jacket at her.

Crystal laid a hand on Julia's arm, stopping her "But we still have inventory... ."

"I'll come in early and take care of it. The Rovers is calling us. You," she said, pointing to Jasmine, "wait here a minute. Crystal, I need a word." Crystal followed Julia into the back office.

Jasmine took a moment to whip off a quick text message, then took the opportunity to look at some of the stock that lined the shelves on the walls and some of the clothing on the circular racks scattered across the floor of the store. She was slightly shocked by the silicone breasts that were directly on her left, and the butt cheeks whose packages were beside them. Jasmine shuddered lightly and went to inspect some sequined tops that caught her eye.

She was casually flipping hangers across their circular rod when she was startled by the low voice behind her.

"Come on," Julia urged, walking towards the front door. "We don't have a lot of time."

"I, ah, I'm heading this way to the train," Jasmine said as they reached the corner. "It was nice to meet you both."

"Oh no you don't. I have orders from your boss lady that you are to come along. And she sounds like someone you don't screw with. So you're coming too."

Jasmine sighed, knowing it was true. If Lucinda said she had to go with them, then go with them she would. She joined Crystal and Julia as they crossed the street.

This is the oddest trio I've ever been part of, Jasmine thought as she walked, flanked by a lesbian and a drag queen. I have *got* to blog this when I get home, she thought with a smile, my friends will never believe the day I've had today. Julia was silent as they strode through the fading spring light. Crystal seemed excited; there was a slight bounce in her step.

Jasmine, though admitting she was buzzed by what she was involved in and curious about where they were going, was for once just anxious to end her workday and get back to her cramped apartment. She was tired of walking, despite her comfortable shoes. She was amazed that Julia had no difficulty handling the fifteen blocks they walked, despite the heels she wore.

Crystal, although she seemed slightly winded as the entered a crowded bar, seemed unfazed. Jasmine saw the tall, brunette bartender give a welcoming nod to Julia, and coquettish wave to Crystal. She felt completely out of place. The bar was filled with men and women obviously finishing up their workday with a martini at the bar before heading home. Jasmine longed for the comforts of her apartment, where she wouldn't see men holding hands, or women discreetly kissing and caressing in a corner booth. She was a Virginia girl at heart: deep down, she had a feeling that, whatever this evening brought, it was going to be way out of her comfort zone.

They ordered from the bar. "Gin and Tonic, heavy on the gin, please," Julia said, her tone dry. Crystal went for bar vodka with a touch of soda.

"Um, I guess I'll have a wine spritzer," Jasmine said, and both Julia and Crystal's eyes snapped to hers. They then looked at each other, and Jasmine could see they were trying not to laugh.

"What?" she said defensively. "What's wrong with that order?"

"No, no. Nothing. It's just very ... well ... I guess the word 'bland' comes to mind." Crystal shrugged. "But if that's what the lady wants, that's what the lady gets."

Their drinks in hand, they snagged a booth some distance from the bar. Julia slipped into the booth first, followed by Crystal. Jasmine had no choice but to slide in across from them both. As soon as she had slipped off her jacket, Crystal excused herself.

"Back in a moment, ladies. I just need a word with the barkeep." She picked up her drink and turned to go.

"You be careful of that one at the bar, Crystal. I've heard some stories."

Crystal laughed. "And if I get lucky, I may be able to confirm them for you tomorrow morning. Time will tell, eh?" She turned and headed to the bar, leaving Julia and Jasmine on their own.

"So tell me about this boss lady of yours, this Lucinda McHauley. What is she like?" Julia asked innocently, taking the two straws that floated on her drink between her lips.

"A bitch," Jasmine said flatly, not even thinking. She raised a hand to cover her mouth. "Sorry. I guess I shouldn't have said that. Besides, I'm only an intern. I've never worked directly for her before. Forget what I said."

Julia waved her concern away, "I'd rather know the truth from someone who works with her, than be surprised while she's sitting across a table from me at a bar. Come on, Jas, tell me some more." Julia leaned in, instilling a sense of camaraderie designed to put Jasmine more at ease.

"Well, she's self-absorbed, she's rude, she's caustic, and most interns – hell, most of her fellow workers – try to steer clear of her. But at the same time, everybody admits she's good. At her job, I mean ... she loves it and she's good. And tough. She means business and will tell it just as it is. She won't bullshit you. In fact, I don't think she has it in her to sugar-coat anything. Ever."

"Interesting," Julia said, placing her drink down on the coaster in front of her. "So what is this meeting all about anyways? You have to know more than you're letting on, and I want to be prepared by the time she gets here."

Jasmine almost spat her drink across the table.

"She's coming here? Oh Jesus! I shouldn't be drinking then. I'm sure that to her, 'company time' is 24/7."

"Honey," Julia said, placing a hand over Jasmine's, "Lucinda wanted to meet here for drinks. She's going to have one, I'm going to have more than one. Now, I don't know why she included you specifically, but I doubt you'll get fired over one measly wine spritzer."

"You don't know Lucinda."

"I know her kind, Jasmine. I know her kind."

∞

As Lucinda's cab pulled up to the curb and she tossed her credit card at the driver, she looked around at the street, swathed in fading light. The hairs on the back of her neck bristled. She couldn't tell if it was the excitement of a plan on the pinnacle of fruition or if someone was scoping her out. Considering the lengths Lucinda had gone to to make this meeting happen, and considering the throngs of smokers huddled outside the bar front doors, it could be either. Storing her credit card back in her wallet, Lucinda made sure her game face was in place and got out of the cab.

Lucinda swung the door to the bar wide and marched inside, scanning the faces huddled around tables as she followed the bar deep into the room. People's gazes were drawn to Lucinda. She was used to it; they couldn't help it. The women in this particular bar all wanted her; the men slightly feared her. It was exactly how she wanted to be perceived. She smiled to herself as she walked up to the bar. She found herself standing next to two women kissing. One, on the customer side of the bar, was quite butchily dressed, and the other was one of the bar staff. Huh, Lucinda thought to herself. I might need to come down here the next... .

She stopped herself right there: she couldn't afford to get sidetracked. She needed to concentrate. She might consider a fling here some time, but this was no time to let in stray thoughts. This was here on business.

"What can I get for you?"

"Screwdriver please; a double."

"Coming up."

When the bartender placed the drink in front of Lucinda, she handed over her AMEX card.

"I'll be running a tab. Have you seen Julia NewMar yet tonight?"

The bartender pocketed the card, and waved a hand toward the back of the bar.

"Yeah, she's in a booth back there."

Lucinda scooped up her drink and headed to the back.

EIGHTEEN

OLIVER SAT back in his chair and tried to make himself as comfortable as possible. 'Phantom of the Opera' played lightly in the background. He tried to clear his mind and enjoy the glass of wine that he dangled in his fingertips. He had much to occupy his thoughts. ISYS, the Foundation, the Company, his Mama. His sister. All were scrambling for their place in the hierarchy of his brain. And he didn't want any of them. Not now, not tonight. He just wanted to enjoy his evening.

He glanced over his shoulder and smiled into the fading sunlight that streamed through his window. Spring. He should be out playing racquetball. He should be over at his Mama's replacing the storm windows with screens. He should be making plans to help his sister; she was a decent kid who was in need of support and direction. Involuntarily, he began assessing the value of the advice he had given Rosella Maria during today's heart-to-heart. Reluctantly, that led him to whether he should be taking his own advice. He should ... the chiming of his doorbell interrupted his thoughts. Thank God.

He didn't bother getting up. He knew who it was, and that she would let herself in. Oliver picked up the remote that lay next to the coaster on the little table besides his chair. He hit one button, silencing the delicate music that wafted through his apartment in time to hear the front door close and the deadbolt be thrown. He heard the clinking of keys being laid next to his, and the unmistakable sound of stilettos, sharp but insinuating, clicking across his entrance hall. He closed his eyes, relishing the sound, feeling the stimulation, his thumbnail absentmindedly picking at the knot of the leather band at his wrist.

"Well, Mr Garcia ... Oliver ... it's been a while," came a voice from across the room. It was a voice of cool neutrality; the hint of warmth it contained might almost be imagined. Oliver needed the warmth to be imagined.

Oliver opened his eyes. She was right where he was expecting her to be, leaning delicately against the wide doorjamb that separated the foyer from the living room. To him, she appeared both provocative and seductive.

"Jasprinder. You're a sight for sore eyes." He kept his voice soft, and slowly stood. "I have missed you."

She shrugged noncommittally, "You haven't broken any fingers and you know how to dial a phone."

"You know it's not that simple." He tried to keep the resignation out of his voice.

"It's as simple as you want it to be, Oliver." she said admonishingly, swinging her waist length braid of ebony hair around over her shoulder. She moved towards him, dropping the coat she wore onto the floor, not caring where it landed. She was dressed simply – part of her *modus operandi* – in kimono blouse and slim skirt. The contradiction to her heritage made her a striking sight. Placing one hand on his chest, she circled around him, her heels muffled on the plush carpeting, allowing her fingers to brush over his torso, arm and back.

Oliver could feel the lack of friction between the silk sleeve of her blouse and the cotton of his button-down shirt. It sent shivers down his spine. He closed his eyes and swallowed deeply, but he didn't turn to where she was standing behind him.

"You know how things are, how things can be." he said, his voice low.

"I'm willing to be what you need right now, love," she said resignedly. "We'll talk later." She moved around to face him, her long fingers reaching to smooth the worry lines along his forehead. His head tipped back, eyes closed and he all but purred at the contact.

"Right now, you clearly need my help." Her dexterous fingers moved to the column of buttons on his shirt, undoing them one by one. "Let's get you to a better place..."

∞

Lucinda spotted Jasmine first, looking very much out of her element, and felt an inkling of pride at her young intern. She had done well today, and sticking it out in a gay bar in the middle of SoHo certainly stepped her up a notch or two in Lucinda's book. And that was saying a lot.

Lucinda presented herself at the booth, and both Jasmine and Julia immediately turned to her. Lucinda thrust her hand towards Julia, introducing herself as she sat down next to Jasmine. She slid a shoe box across the table and Julia took it, tucking it down beside herself.

Lucinda all but ignored the young intern at her side, feeling the need to focus her attention on the woman sitting across from her. The silence at the booth was palpable. Jasmine didn't think it would be possible for her to feel more uncomfortable or out of place. Lucinda and Julia, on the other hand, were using the silence to size each other up. Two strong personalities were present, and it wasn't clear yet who was going to be top dog. Lucinda was prepared to wait it out.

Julia didn't know what to make of the woman sitting across from her in the booth. At a quick assessment, Lucinda was a powerhouse. That much was evident immediately, radiating from her poise, grace and style. Jasmine's assessment appeared to be accurate: Lucinda was used to having things her way, and most certainly wasn't used to having anyone question her authority or expertise. But Lucinda has never met me, Julia thought with a satisfied grin, staring down the petite woman across from her.

While Julia felt the awkward silence, she didn't let it affect her. She was feeling a strength today that she hadn't felt in ages. Heaven help Lucinda MacHauley if she was trying to scam Julia NewMar.

She felt a trace of contempt in Lucinda's gaze. She also sensed Lucinda's hunger. She's hungry for something, Julia thought, something I can provide for her. What in the world could that be? Julia felt her steely gaze falter momentarily and almost spoke, but she stopped herself. Lucinda had gone to a lot of trouble to track her down, and Julia knew that if she played her cards right and this was in fact a legitimate proposition, she couldn't cave now or Lucinda would walk right over her. Julia had nothing to lose at this stage of the game, feeling the box next to her on the seat, so she hunkered down to wait Lucinda out.

It was Jasmine who finally broke the silence.

"So, Lucinda, message delivered." She tried to sound upbeat to cut through the tension at the table. "Very clandestine. The crow flies at midnight and all that." Her voice ended up sounding meeker than she'd intended, and she was rewarded with a withering look from Lucinda.

Julia smiled slightly. Ah, false move, young one. She'll be ticked you said anything. Ouch! Her smile turned into a quick cringe when she witnessed the withering stare that Lucinda gave Jasmine. No need to treat her like that, lady! This little one just doesn't understand the rules! And despite that, she's got you pretty well pegged.

It was all over in a flash, almost as if it hadn't occurred. Lucinda was all business when she turned again to face Julia. Julia just sat there and stared back, her need for strength re-affirmed. Jasmine tried to disappear into her seat and didn't speak again.

Still no real comments had been uttered, though all their drinks were now empty. Crystal had broken away from her entanglement at the bar and headed over to the booth, ready to play her role in Julia's plan.

"So you are Lucinda. The Lady with the Card!" Crystal said as she slid in next to Julia.

Lucinda nodded and held out her hand, noticing that Crystal held it a little bit too long for convention.

"Can I call you Lucy for short?" Crystal asked, a small flirtatious smile playing on her lips.

"No." Lucinda retorted, her eyes narrowing ever so slightly, "there's no future in that." Crystal got the message, loud and clear.

"Point taken." Crystal shifted focus, pointing a thumb at Julia. "So what's so important that you had to send an underling to track down our girl here?" she asked.

Fine, Lucinda thought, I'll cede this first battle and be the first one to speak, "I have some business I'd like to discuss that I think might interest Julia."

"Does this business involve money? Because if we're talking money..." Crystal was stopped by Julia's hand on her arm.

"Do you *want* to talk money first?" Lucinda asked pointedly to Julia, trying to cut Crystal out of the loop. This was getting a bit out of control.

"Do *you* want to talk money first?" Julia retorted, with just a hint of active dislike. At this point, it was a Mexican stand-off.

"Look," Lucinda said, taking a deep breath and leaning in over the table, "I'll go get us another round of drinks and then maybe we'll just start all over again. No bullshit, no games. Just talk. Deal?"

Julia sat back, and nodded slightly, "Deal."

Julia watched Lucinda slide gracefully from the booth and head to the bar. Jesus, she thought, impressed despite herself. This is some tough lady! She then turned to Jasmine, wanting to help her stay in the loop.

"You were right on all counts. But you missed one thing."

Jasmine had been fiddling with the straws in her glass, pushing what remained of the ice cubes around. She stopped and looked at Julia.

"What could I have possibly left off that list?" Jasmine was going over what she'd said about her temporary boss.

"I guess it's not important for the working relationship you have with her. But I like her. We have a lot in common, the two of us. I can speak her language, and she senses that. I don't think she quite knows what to make of me. But I'll hear her out. I'm curious now."

"Why the silence then? Why the staring competition?"

Crystal guffawed, and chimed in, "Man, you are a young one. This is the female equivalent of a pissing contest," she continued when she saw that Jasmine wasn't getting it, "To see who is going to be in charge. Who is going to call the shots." She sighed in frustration, "To see who is going to be in control of this business arrangement."

"Oh," Jasmine said, and went back to fiddling with the ice in her glass. She was an unhappy camper; she'd just been put down by Lucinda and mocked by a lesbian. On top of that, her feet hurt, and all she really wanted was to go home.

"Jasmine," Julia said softly, "If you can buck up, suck it up enough, you might pay attention to your boss lady. You will learn more than a thing or two about business – the what to do and what not to do. She's set her path, and from what I've heard from you, it works for her. I doubt the same path would work for you, but you could certainly gain some experience from her."

"Yeah, experience on how to be the bitchiest bitch out of the bunch."

"People perceive strength as bitchiness, and quite often women use their bitchiness as a cover for lack of strength. I don't think that's the case with our Lucinda. She's strong and she's a bitch. Forget the bitchiness. Learn her strength."

∞

Lucinda strode up to the bar, ignoring the glances from those around her. She leaned into the counter and was startled to feel two firm hands on her hips, and hot breath in her ear.

"You've been ignoring my calls." Her spine stiffened but she didn't turn around.

"You missed our dates, I missed your calls. That's how these things work, Hank."

The bartender passed Lucinda by, completing other orders. Hank's fingers bit a bit deeper into her sides. She smacked his hands away and spun on him.

"You don't get to touch anymore. You don't get to whisper anymore. Not now."

"Lucy – "

"And you most certainly don't get to call me Lucy anymore!"

"Would you rather I call you Mistress?" He said with a smile which was promptly wiped from his face by the scathing look Lucinda threw his way.

"I've been worried about you." This time, his sincerity was evident. He clearly meant it.

"Not worried enough to make our dates, apparently. I don't get stood up, Hank. Not by you. Not by anybody. Find yourself a more willing playmate."

"What the hell, Lucy. I told you there was a good chance I was going away for work and wouldn't make our date. You said okay."

"Don't call me that," she said tightly. "I'm working."

She turned back to the bar hoping to catch the bartender's attention. She could not recall the conversation about Hank going away at all. She couldn't have forgotten, could she?

Again, she felt his breath in her ear. "You're Lucy with me. The same Lucy whose pig-tails I used to pull. The one and the same who didn't go to prom because she didn't have a date. The Lucy who shot guns with her brothers for fun, but couldn't empty a mousetrap."

She spun back towards him, eyes wide. "You remember that?"

"Lucy, I remember everything about you. I was just too chicken shit around your older brothers to ask you out. I was crazy about you then, and I'm crazy about you now. I'm sorry you felt I stood you up. I really was out of town. I hope you can believe that."

She looked into his eyes and saw his sincerity, and – for a moment, at least – wanted to believe it, to let her hard shell crack a little bit.

"I mean it, Hank. I really can't do this now. But you're right. We need to talk." It was said almost as a whisper.

"Yes we do."

"Not now, I'm working."

"Later tonight?" He was hopeful.

"A couple of days, maybe … work… ."

"And if I call, you'll answer?"

"Yes. I will answer." She turned back to the bar and gave her order to the waiting bartender.

"I'm not going anywhere."

"You're wrong," she said over her shoulder. "You are going to go home. I have work to do."

"Okay, I will." He said pressing a quick kiss to her temple as she signed to update the tab.

"I've missed all of you, Lucy. Now get your Lucinda face back on and kick some royal business deal ass."

She felt his presence leave her back, and as she laid the pen gently on the sticky bar top, she glanced back at the booth, her eyes catching those of Jasmine, who looked almost gleefully over the rim of her empty wine glass. Oh Christ, thought Lucinda. I hope she can't read lips!

∞

Lucinda came back with her hands filled with drinks. She placed them down on the table-top and divvied them up. She sat with a slight sigh.

"So, Lucinda, what did you want to ask Julia about?" the young intern piped in, her gaze skipping between the two headstrong women in front of her.

"All right. Business." She ignored Jasmine and Crystal, directing her comments to Julia alone. "I'm going to tell you about a concept I'm developing, and outline what I hope will be your part in it."

Julia nodded and took a sip of the drink in front of her.

"Manolo Blahnik has been one of the top sellers of women's footwear for the last three years. Jimmy Choo is fast and furiously on our tail. So, as part of my job in Research and Development, I've been thinking of ways to expand our business. Areas, markets that have been under-utilized or underdeveloped. That is where you come in. I would like to see Manolo Blahnik start a Men's Line of Women's shoes."

Julia felt her breath catch, and knew from the flicker in Lucinda's eyes that she had caught it too.

"You know from your work as a performer how a comfortable shoe is important. Women's shoes, even in the larger sizes that would fit the length of your foot, are often too narrow. So, you would have to either suffer with the pinching or get shoes custom made. The first option isn't comfortable, and the second is expensive. And for some of our male clients, either awkward to explain or embarrassing to have fitted. Not all men can afford to let their love of women's shoes be known.

Still, if a man is willing to spend the money to have his shoes custom made, copying Manolo's styles, Manolo Blahnik might as well start making them and selling them to guarantee workmanship and all of that other business stuff you don't need to worry about."

Lucinda could see Julia nodding in understanding, so she continued.

"So that's the plan I'd like to bring to our Marketing Department meeting on Wednesday. I'd like to bring to them a few ideas on ad designs," Lucinda reached down and pulled some sketches she'd hacked out while waiting for Jasmine to call earlier, "similar to these. I also want to suggest a runway show using drag queens – that's where you come in. And depending on what Marketing has to say, I'd like to get this all done before Manolo's Autumn season starts."

Julia put down her drink, folded her hands together, and thought for a moment.

"So my part would be to suggest or find queens to be in your ads? Hardly seems worthwhile tracking me down for that."

"No, Julia. That wouldn't just be your part, although I'd love to get your help with that. I'd like you to be the focal queen in all our ads. It could be you solo, or you with one or two others: that's probably a Marketing decision. Here. Take a look through these sketches."

Lucinda shoved the papers across to Julia, who in turn picked them up and flipped through them. Very interesting concepts, Julia thought, and I would get to be in all of these? She could feel her heart start beating faster, with excitement and anticipation.

Lucinda waited a moment before she spoke, allowing the sketches to grab hold of Julia's imagination.

"What I'd like to do, and mind you this is all up in the air until I get approval from Marketing, is have you come in as a Creative Director – in name only. And it would be for this promotion only. You wouldn't have all the duties and responsibilities a Creative Director would normally carry on a campaign like this, but we'd have to give you some sort of title to justify the pay."

Julia sifted through the sketches one more time. She was intrigued by the proposal Lucinda had just briefly outlined. She was intrigued by the concept of drag queens becoming more mainstream. From what Lucinda had implied this was not a minor ad campaign, and that made Julia excited.

"So if I do decide to help you with this..." Julia started.

Crystal piped in, cutting Julia off, "Aren't you even a little bit curious about the moola, Jules?"

"It wouldn't matter how curious either of you are," Lucinda said, tenting her fingers under her chin, "Marketing hasn't even approved the concept yet, let alone the ad campaign. I have no budget, I have no approvals for anything yet. Once I wow them at the meeting on Wednesday, I'll have a better idea of where this can go, and how big we can take it, thus how much we can pay as salary or fee, Julia. But what I was hoping you could do is start thinking of people in your circle, people you perform with, legends, up-and-comers. Start compiling a list of people you think – now that you've seen the sketches – would be interested or would 'fit' the ideas of the ads. Once we get approval, we are going to have to move quickly on this."

Julia nodded, understanding. She didn't really need the money. This wasn't about the money or the prestige. This was about bringing her lifestyle, the one so newly chosen, out into the forefront of mainstream society.

"So, Julia?" Lucinda asked as quietly as she could over the melee of conversations in the bar, "What do you think?"

Julia didn't need to think this through. She felt her answer in her gut. And she trusted her gut. "I think you have a deal. I'll get started on the list tonight." She held her hand across the table and Lucinda met Julia's grip half way. Their handshake was solid.

"You'll be in touch tomorrow, I assume?" Julia asked, waving Crystal out of the booth.

"Yes. I'd like to get some names and pictures from the internet that I can take into this meeting. I'll give you a call in the late afternoon, I'm out of the office just after lunch."

"Fine." Julia said, slipping on her jacket. She stopped and breathed deeply. "Well. Lucinda. It was a pleasure to meet you." Julia turned to Jasmine and leaned in across the end of the booth table. "And you, Jasmine, you'll do fine. Keep strong." She started to walk backwards away from them.

"Good night ladies." she said with a wave, then turned, and with Manolo Blahnik shoe bag swinging, was followed by Crystal out of the bar.

"Well, Jasmine," Lucinda said to her intern, "I think your day is finally over. Thank you for finding Julia."

"I'm glad I could help. And I've learned a lot, too. It's been an interesting day, Lucinda. I don't think I'll forget it for a long, long time."

"Oh, you'll remember it all right," she said, smiling and polishing off her drink. "Come on, we should get going. Tomorrow is going to be another busy day. Oh and Jasmine?" Lucinda said, turning to Jasmine as she slipped out of the booth, "I don't think I have to say this but I will anyways,

just in case: don't mention this campaign around the office.
You know I would make your life a living hell at the office if I
were to get scooped because you've got loose lips."

"No, I won't say anything," Jasmine said, slipping on her
jacket. "You have my word on that."

"Okay then. I'll see you in the morning." Lucinda turned
and strode out of the bar, leaving before she could see Jasmine
putting on her own coat and giving Hank a discreet hi-five
where he was huddled at the bar before heading out into the
New York night alone.

NINETEEN

OLIVER'S BREATH started to regulate itself as he rolled over from his stomach onto his back. He winced slightly as he did so, despite the plush carpeting, and smiled to himself. He turned his head so he could see Jassy, now sitting on the couch. Her hair had become unbound at some point, and having abandoned doing up her blouse at about the half-way point, she was now re-braiding her long locks into a thick plait.

Oliver's gaze followed from Jassy's pristine face over her silken shoulders and the unbound breasts he could see through her blouse. From his angle on the ground he couldn't see if she had put on her skirt yet, but he had a glorious view of her silken calves and painted toes as they poked through the straps of her Jimmy Choo strappy sandals.

Oliver closed his eyes as he remembered those same sandals walking their way up his back, causing each vertebrae to snap back into alignment. He rolled his shoulders, the discomfort he felt paling in comparison to the thrill of debauchery. He could almost pinpoint the spots up and down his spine where each heel had ground into his skin. He had no clue how he was going to explain the marks, the probable bruising, to his chiropractor tomorrow, but right now he didn't care. He'd felt the love of Jassy. Jassy and her Jimmy Choos. His eyes flickered up, and caught her curious gaze.

"Oliver?" Her deep voice was such a contradiction to her petite size. "What on earth is going through your mind right now? You just had the oddest expression cross your face." She leaned over him, her hands gliding gently over his chest, drawing him out of his daze.

Oliver took a deep breath and rubbed his face into the pillow under his cheek. "I'm reveling in your talent, love. My back feels marvelous. And no broken skin, eh?"

"Nope. You taught me well. I hope I did right."

Oliver tightened his stomach muscles, arching his lower back further into the carpeting, "Yes, darling, you did a fabulous job."

Jassy stood slowly, walking the short distance to where the short skirt she had been wearing was now pooled on the floor. As she walked around the couch, she did up the last few buttons of her blouse and tied the sash, then scooped up the jacket from where it had been dropped onto the floor next to the couch. She sashayed to it and sat, turning back toward Oliver where he still lay on the carpet.

"Are you sure you wouldn't like to have some supper with me, Oliver? You've got to be hungry after all that." She got a grumbled response. "How about take away? I can call the Thai place on the corner you like." Her voice dropped to almost a whisper, "I don't want to leave you like this."

"I'll be fine, dear Jas. Truly. I'll have a long hot bath, whip up some soup and have an early night. I've taken up too much of your time already; you should probably go."

She sighed. She wasn't surprised that she'd been so swiftly dismissed. That was Oliver's M.O. She just had to savour the time they did get to spend together, albeit too brief and infrequent for her tastes. "I'll leave the balms on your bedside table as per normal then," she said, slipping into the other room.

"Of course, Jassy." Oliver said, propping himself up on his elbows. "I appreciate you squeezing me into your schedule."

She re-entered the room and slipped on her jacket. "I'm here for you." She walked towards where he was still lying near the window. "I will always be here for you." She knelt beside him for a brief second and placed a gentle kiss on the side of his lips. "I love you Oliver. All of you."

His eyes met hers, and softened, "Jasprinder… ."

"I know, I know." She stood again, looking down on him, "I won't press." She crossed to the front door, turning back to him when her fingers grasped the handle. "Don't wait so long, Oliver. I'm here to listen as well – talk to me before things go so far."

All she could hear was a grunted response as he rolled over within the blanket. "I love you." she said quietly, slipping out as quickly as she'd arrived.

Oliver relished the silence for a few seconds, then felt her absence. "I love you too, Jasprinder Singh." Dammit, he really *should* be taking his own advice.

∞

Julia parted company with Crystal shortly after they left the bar. Crystal was bound and determined to hook up with that bartender, despite Julia's warnings, so she had doubled back into the darkness. Julia, head filled with possibilities, was actually relieved to have silence. She needed to think.

Lucinda, Julia determined, was certainly prepared. The images from the sketches swam in front of her eyes. This was a very interesting proposition. And with Julia's connections in the cross-dressing world, it wasn't surprising that she had been chosen. Julia felt her shoulders straighten a bit with pride. She was in demand – more than just for her performing. She laughed out loud and found her step had an added spring to it as she headed towards the subway.

Now, sitting across the dining room table from his parents, having divested himself of Julia for the evening, Julian found it easy to tune out their bickering. Tonight they were on about where to celebrate Passover. Julian couldn't care less.

His head was filled with the bright lights and backdrops he imagined were involved in any photo shoot. He tucked a tendril of hair that had escaped his pony tail behind his ear. He wanted to get up to his computer and start compiling names. He wanted to go and research Lucinda. He wanted to know what truly made her tick. When will dessert be over with, he wondered, pushing the remnants of his apple pie around his plate. He looked up to his parents, who were still eating but were oblivious to the fact he was even sitting at the table. Silently, he pushed his chair back, picked up his plate and empty coffee cup, and headed into the kitchen.

He had some decisions to make, he realized. He'd made one big one already today, but this was different. He adored his parents. They had been as supportive as any with his metamorphoses over the years. They hadn't batted an eye at any overnight guests he'd had over the years, including any partner he'd chosen to include in their familial breakfasts or suppers. But Julian was 25 years old, and for the first time he felt the overwhelming desire to move away from home.

He shook his head and scraped the last of his apple pie into the trash. Placing his dishes in the dishwasher, Julian made a tentative plan. It was contingent on Lucinda and her ad campaign. Mind whirling, Julian headed down the hall and up the narrow staircase to his room.

∞

Lucinda let herself into her apartment with a satisfied sigh. She had had a good day. She placed her briefcase and purse just inside the doorway, and put her keys on the table next to the front door. She kicked off the mocha brown heels and left them toppled under the table. She was due a night off.

She wandered through her place, flicking on light switches as she went, and headed into the bathroom to run a scalding soak. The blinking light of her answering machine stopped her dead in her tracks. She knew without pressing the 'play' button who it would be. She felt her stomach dip towards her toes, but not allowing the dread to build, she went over and listened to the message.

"Lucy? It's Hank. I'm just heading over to Rovers, a little birdie told me you'd be there tonight – hoping to talk to you. So by the time you get this message, you've either forgiven me or aren't talking to me and are burning my likeness in ceremonial fires. Personally I hope it's the former." Lucinda grinned despite herself.

Lucinda crossed her arms, feeling the grin turn into a slight frown and the tension knot between her shoulder blades tighten. The next message played.

"I know you said a couple of days, but I've missed you and I'm horrible at following orders. I'm going to be in your neck of the city tomorrow. Will you meet me for a drink? Perhaps we can play afterwards? Let me know. If you got the flowers, you have my new number. If somehow or other you 'lost' the card included with the flowers, my new cell number is... ."

Lucinda listened to the end of his message, fingers hovering over the 'erase' button on her machine, unusually hesitant. Somehow, the earth's axis seemed to have tilted just a little bit after the unexpected, hurried exchange at the bar in Rovers, and she didn't know how to deal with what the new rules might imply.

While her bath was filling, Lucinda paced. She couldn't seem to settle herself or her thoughts. She berated herself for wanting to call Hank. Certainly, she'd deleted his old phone numbers from her phone, but she couldn't delete the new one from her mind. She picked up the phone twice without dialing, the memory of their time together swimming in her brain. Hank was indeed a lovely man. They'd had many good times together. Good nights together was more like it, Lucinda thought, but the potential for good days as well was becoming more evident.

But it wasn't a relationship they had, she tried to justify to herself. They were playmates; adult playmates. Just as they had been *childhood* playmates back in Iowa. There could be no present tense. She couldn't risk a real relationship, could she? Could she really have found someone who could cherish the Lucy and still respect the Lucinda? Could she ever be that lucky?

She walked into her bedroom and opened her closet. She unzipped her skirt and let it slide to the floor, sidestepping it without looking. She unbuttoned her blouse and let it drop into the dry cleaning pile at the bottom of her closet. Her delicates placed in the laundry pile, Lucinda padded into the bathroom and eased herself into the hot bath.

She shoved all thoughts of Hank aside, and as she lay back in the hot water, allowing the steam to waft about her, she imagined herself in front of the Marketing staff and visualized how well she would sell her brilliant idea.

∞

Oliver sat under his big living room window and smoked a cigarette. He rarely smoked, but tonight it seemed fitting. Although his visit with Jassy today had filled a need in him, it was fleeting. Only hours later he was left feeling alone, with only a satisfyingly uncomfortable sting coursing up his back. This wasn't how it usually was. Usually he could carry the images, the feel of Jassy with him for up to days at a time after a visit. But not tonight. Tonight he was left empty, and he didn't like it one little bit.

Jasprinder accepted his kink. She accepted him for who he was, wrinkles and all. Why couldn't he reciprocate? Was he so shallow as to let her ethnicity matter? Was he too afraid of what his Mama would say? God, what a coward! He groaned and ran a rough hand over his face. He leaned forward, allowing the cool breeze from the open window to play across his sensitive back. He sighed, feeling the familiar tension resting between his hips. He'd been hoping that Jassy would knock his vertebrae back into order, but that too had failed. He couldn't avoid going to see Dr Warshinsk now, despite the marks on his back. He'd wear one of the undershirts he saved for just such an occasion, he determined, as he stubbed out the cigarette and stood carefully.

He stretched cautiously and headed over to his desk in his office. After switching on the small desk lamp, he sat, hit the start-up button on his machine and took a deep breath. There was no ritual he felt like tonight. He just wanted comfort. The only thing he could think of that might possibly fill the acute loneliness and loathing he felt tonight was a trusted old friend. He opened up the bottom drawer of his desk and pulled out the shoe box that lay at the back. He placed the closed box beside his keyboard and thought for a moment. He inspected the box as he did every time, and found nothing had been disturbed. He gingerly lifted the lid and gazed at his beauties. The leather still gleamed, the heels were hardly worn, yet he'd had these shoes for nearly three years.

Oliver didn't bother with music. He didn't bother with stockings or make up, he just withdrew the first shoe and held it in the palm on his hand. Yes, he thought, they had served him well. But perhaps it was time to move on. To expand his fetish or to let it go. Perhaps he could allow himself a second indulgence or perhaps a different one altogether. These pumps had been his saving grace through many a hard time, but tonight, they hardly felt enough to fill the void.

He slipped the first one onto his foot. Oliver tried to wiggle his toes, the pinching oddly satisfying him. The second shoe shortly followed. He stood, and walked back out to the living room and grabbed the phone from its cradle. He sauntered back into the office and sat, tucking his legs under his chair and daintily crossing his ankles. He swiveled slightly in his chair and began logging into the Manolo Blahnik website. Perhaps this would bolster his confidence, help him to actually grow a set and call her.

TWENTY

LUCINDA WOKE earlier than her alarm and felt oddly nervous. She had some fine-tuning to do in preparation for tomorrow's Marketing meeting. Julia's list of possible queens would have to be vetted; her data presentation could be ramped a bit. She might even try to tighten her own presentation's focus. She could leave Jasmine to ride herd on Julia if necessary – she should be able to handle at least that task – and still have lots of time for the chiropractor. Dr Warshinsk would be a piece of cake. The Marketing meeting? Not so much. When she thought through all the prep work she'd gone over last night while soaking in the bath, something felt off. It was out of character for her to second guess an approach, especially one that she'd taken so much time and energy to arrange. She took a few minutes, idling in bed, mentally attacking other approaches to this all-important meeting.

"Enough!", she muttered to herself as she rolled out of bed and padded, naked, into the kitchen. Hot mug of coffee in hand, she returned to her closet, and swung the door wide. She wanted to chose her clothing with care today. The right impression would need to be made. Very 'don't mess with me I know what I'm talking about' and 'I dare you to turn me down'. Leather, she thought to herself, pulling out of her closet a simple moss green leather miniskirt. She pulled out a fitted black leather shirt as well, and held it above the skirt, inspecting 'the look'. She replaced the leather top back on the clothing rod. It looked far too dominant. She pulled out a cream, fitted, silk knit v-necked sweater. Yes, she thought, with cream opaque hose and cream pumps. Perfect. Lucinda took a quick gulp of her coffee, put the cup down on her dresser and headed into the bathroom for a quick shower.

∞

As soon as Oliver's eyes opened, he regretted having Jassy over the night before. His back burned like a son of a bitch, and he'd slept poorly because of it. He switched off the alarm that was blaring on his bedside table, grimacing as the cotton of his sheets rubbed against his spine. Normally he'd still be reveling in the pain. He'd use it as a motivator, he'd wear clothing purposefully to inflame. But not today.

He had new clients to meet with so he could bid on a construction job for a strip mall developer, and he had to see Dr Warshinsk this afternoon. All Oliver really wanted was to crawl back under the covers and lie on his stomach for a while. He was tired. Tired of his same old routine. Tired of his jobs. It saddened him to realize it, but he was even tired of his one pair of heels. He wanted new, he wanted excitement, and he wanted a woman in his life who fit. Why was it so difficult to find his ideal?

Then he thought about his back, his hidden womens' shoes, his clandestine makeup, his stay-up stockings. Were those more than the accoutrements of his private fantasy world? Was he twisted in some way? Was this a sickness? No woman in her right mind would want to be party to this, would she? God in heaven, how could even consider finding his ideal woman?

He sighed, stood, and wandered towards his closet. When he opened the door, his suits all looked old to him, his ties, uninspiring. Everything was just so bloody familiar. He removed from its hanger a dark brown light worsted suit, and tossed it on the bed. A light pinstriped shirt followed, and then a simple silk tie. He slipped over to his dresser and grabbed an undershirt from the top left hand drawer. He hated wearing them, even though his father wore one every day of his life. For Oliver, they equated to poverty and deprivation.

He hadn't been able to bring himself to look in the mirror last night before his shower. In the light of day it would be worse; the marks would be too stark, even against his olive skin. He shuddered lightly and placed the shirt over his head, pulling it gingerly over his torso. He pulled on some boxer shorts and headed into the kitchen.

Coffee mug in hand, Oliver returned to his room and started dressing. He felt no energy, no kick from the caffeine his travel mug held. He just felt listless. And his back hurt.

∞

Julia was finishing her eyeliner application when there was a tap on her bathroom door. Her father's face peered around the corner.

"Morning, Julia. Um, your mother's out of the house early, and I'm just about to leave myself, so I wanted you to know you were on your own for breakfast."

"Fine, Dad. Thanks." Julia replied, not looking away from the mirror.

Her father hesitated, then finally spoke, "Is everything all right, Julia? You've been awfully quiet since the picnic. I mean, your mother has told me about Christophe. I'm sorry about that, but ... well ... everything else is ok? Do you need money?"

Julia put down the eyeliner and turned to her father, so she was leaning back against the counter top.

"Dad, everything is fine. Really. I'm kind of making some changes to my life. But don't worry, I'll sit down and talk with you and Mom about it soon enough. Right now I'm still processing. Don't worry though, really. Everything is fine."

"If you say so. I mean, Julia, I know that lately your mother and I have been spending a lot of time at each other's throats. But we're still here for you. You just have to tell us to shut up for a minute."

Julia chuckled. "Yeah, Dad. Right. I'll remember to do that over the dinner table."

"Okay, I grant you that's not the easiest thing in the world to do. I mean it, though. Just snap us back into reality. Please."

Julia turned back to the mirror and resumed her application. "I will Dad. Have a good day, I'll see you at supper tonight."

"Right – o."

Julia smiled to herself. It was going to be difficult to leave her parents. She really did love them to bits, despite their idiosyncrasies. She wished all the young gays she saw in the shop each day had such support in their corner. But after work today she was going to go looking for an apartment on her own. It didn't have to be big, but it did need a large bathroom, she determined, looking about her own and loving the size. And closet space. It needed lots of closet space. She put her makeup away and headed down to make herself some breakfast.

∞

Oliver was dragging. He couldn't seem to get any sort of pep into his step this morning. He contemplated briefly grabbing a third cup of coffee to drink on his way to work, but decided against it. He was late enough as it was. He tossed his suit jacket over his arm, snagged his keys from the table beside the front door and headed out. The second mug of coffee he'd guzzled back before leaving had done little to wake him up. He just felt wired and dopey. He fidgeted with his keys as he was waiting for the elevator to arrive.

Oliver was swinging his keys on his fingers as the car descended towards the parking level. He was startled when the elevator chimed and came to a stop, causing his keys to go spinning off his fingers and fall with a loud clatter to the elevator floor. Oliver stooped to pick them up and as he started to rise, The Shoes entered the elevator again. Oliver stopped mid-stoop, causing his back to spasm slightly. He grabbed his back, groaned and stood slowly and gingerly, taking in the woman attached to the wonderful legs and gorgeous beige pumps. If his breath hadn't been knocked out of him by the spasm of pain coursing across his back, it certainly would have been by the vision that stood next to him in the elevator.

Oliver discreetly gave the young woman a once-over. She couldn't have been more than 5'2", she was compact, and looked strong despite her height. From the top of her short black cropped hair to the tip of her Manolo Blahnik heels, she was the image of perfection in his eyes. He bowed his head and stared at the shoes she wore again. Oh, he thought, they must be a size 6. Those shoes were perfect for the outfit, perfect for the woman. His gaze traveled up her stockinged legs, and despite the long beige coat she had draped over her arm, he could see a bit of her short green skirt, the beige top she wore with its plunging V-neck, and the single gold chain that she had around her long, graceful neck. When Oliver finally got to look at the face that topped the ideal body for him, he was faced with eyes darker than night, and just as fierce.

"Getting a good enough look?" she asked, her voice cool.

"Um, ah." Oliver stuttered, and was appalled that he could allow himself to be caught so flagrantly sizing someone up. "Sorry, I was just ... um..." He seemed to lose his train of thought as a blush infused him, burning his cheeks and ears. She quirked her head to one side, allowing her gaze to size him up in return.

"You were just..." she started again for him. Although her tone softened slightly, her eyes were cold as ice, full of disdain.

The elevator chimed its arrival at the lobby, saving Oliver from any further humiliation. Legs got off the elevator, and as the doors closed, so did Oliver's eyes as he heard her heels click away along the foyer tiles. Oliver swallowed hard, his heart racing, and vowed to take the stairs every day in the future so he would never have to see that look in her eye again.

Lecherous bastard, Lucinda thought as she strode through the foyer, you probably just wanted the shoes. It took her half a block before she stopped dead in her tracks. My God! That little worm wasn't lusting after me. He was hot and bothered over my shoes! She laughed to herself and continued towards the subway.

∞

Oliver was still shaken when he walked into Garcia Construction. He had to pull it together for this string of morning meetings. Business, he thought, not shoes ... business, not shoes. Susan was waiting for him as he swung the front doors of the office open and walked through.

"They're all here. You're late." she said, walking beside him, taking his coat, and handing him the file folder that had all the specs in it. "Rossi is grumpy, and I overheard that Portobello Construction has bid on this one as well. From what I can gather, they've undercut our bid, so you're going to need to work some magic in there, Oliver."

Oliver just nodded, and headed into the boardroom. "Gentlemen, I'm sorry to have kept you waiting..."

∞

Lucinda was still smiling when she entered the offices of Manolo Blahnik. But her smile died on her face when she rounded the corner to her office and found Jasmine waiting for her. The look on Jasmine's face was not happy.

"Jesus, Lucinda, where have you been? I've been calling your cell for the last half an hour."

"Jasmine?" Lucinda warned as she unlocked her office, and walked inside, hitting the light switch as she went. "We've been through this before. What time is it? Do I have my coat off? And a coffee in my hand? Are you a slow learner?"

Jasmine waved off the threat, following Lucinda into her office. This wasn't the time to play by Lucinda's rules.

"Lucinda, just listen! I happened to be in early and overheard the VP of Marketing in the staff room. They've pulled tomorrow's Marketing meeting up to 9:30 this morning. "

Lucinda stopped in her tracks, plunked her briefcase on her chair, and draped her coat over the back. "The bastards!" Lucinda whispered, unaware that she'd muttered out loud.

"Are they trying to scoop you? Because I swear, I said nothing. I haven't talked to..."

Lucinda cut her off, only half hearing her, and madly started pulling files out of her desk drawer with one hand while booting up her lap top with the other.

"No, this has nothing to do with scooping. And I trust I put the fear of God into you about talking. This has to do with Stuartson. That bastard knew something was up when ... well, not your concern. He wants me out, and he thinks he can catch me off guard." Lucinda put her briefcase on the floor and sat, typing frantically on her keyboard.

"Okay, Jasmine. This is what we're going to do. You'd better sit down, and take some notes," Lucinda said, shoving a thick pad of paper across her desk.

∞

When Crystal walked in, Julia was half sitting, half propping herself on the stool behind the counter. She had two papers open on the top of the cabinet, and three others stacked waiting their turn. The classifieds were open in both papers, and Julia was monotonously reading each and every ad, twiddling a red pen between her elegant fingers.

"Whatcha doing?" Crystal asked, peeking over Julia's shoulder.

"You're late." Julia replied, circling the third ad on that page.

"Are you job hunting, girl?" Crystal said, scanning the papers. "No you're looking for an apartment! Good Lord! Are you finally moving out of mommy and daddy's place?" She stood back, a mocking look in her eye. "Awww, look at how my little girl has grown up!"

"Enough, Crystal," Julia said, irritated at her friend's tone. "There's work to be done. Those deliveries still need to be completed. They're waiting for you in the back."

Crystal pursed her lips and headed towards the back of the store.

Julia yelled after her, "Oh! How was your night last night? Did you get your heart broken?"

Crystal turned and smiled wickedly at her old friend, "Honey, it wasn't my *heart* that got broken..."

Julia smiled and returned to her classified ads, and was interrupted almost immediately by the phone ringing.

"Bras, Belts and Boas."

"Julia NewMar, please."

"Speaking."

"Julia? Lucinda here. Sorry to call so early, but there has been a slight change in scheduling. Do you have any names compiled yet for people you think would work in our ad campaign?"

"Well, yes, I have an idea of who to use. But I haven't gathered any pictures or anything yet. I thought I had until this afternoon."

"Yes, well, so did I." Lucinda's voice was dry, and did not invite further comment on the matter.

"Oh. Okay. Did you want me to...?"

"Names, Julia," Lucinda interrupted. "Given the change in deadline I'll have to make do with names. Can you text or fax at least that much to me?"

"The names aren't entered on this computer. And our fax machine is down right now – typical small business issue. I can give you the names of the people I've been considering over the phone, but I haven't pulled any bios on them yet. That's about the best I can do right now."

"Start talking. We'll have to go with what you've got. We can fine-tune later if we have to."

"First and foremost, Sophia LaRiche. She's been the leader in our community for the last 25 years." Julia put her pen down, not needing to look at the list she had tucked in her jacket pocket. "Second would be Wilhemina Nomana... ."

∞

Five minutes later, Lucinda had the best names Julia could offer. The list was woefully short, and had virtually no details. She tore the sheet off her writing pad and handed the sheet to Jasmine.

"Okay, I need as much information on these people as you can get in the next ... bloody hell, twenty-five minutes. No time to get it into presentation shape, but find whatever you can. Focus on appearance, breadth of appeal, performance history ... anything suggesting their ability to draw and hold a crowd. Meet me at Boardroom 'C' at 9:30 with whatever you can dig up. We'll go in there with guns blazing."

Jasmine gulped. "You want me in this meeting too?"

"You have to learn sometime, Jasmine. And I like the way you've responded here. Although if anyone were to ask me if I really said that, I'd deny it." Lucinda gave Jasmine a rare smile.

Jasmine squared her shoulders proudly. "Okay, I'll get on it. I'll see you in 20 minutes at the boardroom." And she rushed out of the office to her cubicle with questions still unasked.

Lucinda hunched over her keyboard and started hammering out a revised proposal. The background data was not compromised, thank God, but going on the "do the best with what you've got" principle, Julia gradually became a larger focal point of the ad campaign than Lucinda had imagined. When you only know one queen, you build around her strengths. By the time she had finished her revision, Lucinda actually thought it might be tighter than the one she had had to discard. Maybe Stuartson's attempted sabotage would backfire on him. This was the kind of pressure she thrived on.

TWENTY-ONE

WHEN JASMINE rushed up to the doors of Boardroom 'C', Lucinda was waiting, looking as calm, cool, and fierce as ever. Jasmine quickly handed over a dozen printed sheets. A few were pictures, Lucinda discovered as she skimmed through them, but mostly they were resume-type biographies. It was far from what she'd hoped for, but better than she expected. Not Jasmine's fault, Lucinda thought, and the lack of detail couldn't be covered at the 11th hour. She turned to open the doors to the boardroom, but stopped and offered Jasmine a tight smile.

"They're going to jump all over me, like hyenas on a carcass. That's their weakness: they don't expect me to fight back, let alone launch an offensive. But believe me, we're walking into a war zone.

"Don't say a thing while you're in there. Sit on my right side if you can, and keep that pile of stuff you just dug up in front of you. I talk; you observe. Follow what I'm saying. If I raise an issue and you think something in your pile would support it, dig it out. But be unobtrusive; I may not need it. Watch and learn, Jasmine. Watch and learn."

Jasmine had only an inkling of what that was all about, it came so out of the blue. Were those instructions or advice? But she nodded, and followed her leader into the boardroom.

"Gentlemen," Lucinda started as soon as she'd crossed the threshold. She found Stuartson sitting at the head of the table and stared down at his smarmy, gloating face as she found a pair of unclaimed seats. She sat and placed a single file in front of her, hoping Jasmine had the brains to follow her hasty instructions. Judging by the faces around the table, this would indeed be a battle. Without opening her file, she commenced firing.

"I want to thank you for moving this meeting forward. There have been recent rumours, I know, that R&D staff were preparing a proposal for your consideration. Moving this meeting to this morning gives me a chance to put the rumours to rest." Lucinda paused, taking a brief sip of water.

"This morning, I'm delighted to place my proposal before you. It's daring. It's innovative. It's industry leading. And it's going to set the shoe world on its ear... ."

∞

Oliver sat down heavily at his desk and thumped the bundle of file folders he'd been carrying in front of him. The meeting had been a disaster. He'd botched it like an inexperienced salesman. He'd been unable to focus throughout the whole thing, losing his train of thought, unable to do simple math equations in his head, missing chances at counter-proposals. A disaster, that's what he'd been! Useless!

He was certain that Portobello Construction was going to win the contract for the strip mall. It pissed him off no end that he'd basically handed his closest competitor such a lucrative contract. Had an employee made such an inept presentation, Oliver would have fired him on the spot.

He sighed heavily and flipped open the top file. Even now, he wasn't seeing the figures listed on the printouts on the bid he'd blown. He wasn't even feeling the tight burning that seared it's way up his back, now just a nagging reminder of last night's indulgence. He was seeing beige pumps. Beige pumps with beige hose. He sighed and gave his head a shake, picking up his phone.

"Susan? Hold my calls, please." She probably didn't need to ask why.

But when he booted up his computer, he headed straight to the Manolo site. A worry about why he needed the site at that precise moment crossed his mind, but that didn't stop him from hitting that 'enter' key and getting transported out of reality for a while.

∞

Julia hung up the phone as Crystal walked out of the back office. She ripped one page out of the classifieds section of the newspaper, and folded the rest neatly.

"All done back there?" Julia asked, tucking the paper into her small clutch.

"Yes, no thanks to you." Crystal grumbled.

"What do you expect when you show up late for work? You have the capability, Crystal, you just need the dedication."

"I was hardly late at all. Five minutes, tops, on the outside, maybe."

Julia shook her head. "You need to be here early if you want to start managing this store."

"Managing? Me?"

Julia sighed contentedly. "Crystal, I'm not going to be here forever. Someone is going to have to take the reins. If you're interested, you've got an inside track. If you're interested, you'll have to step up."

"But, well, I'd never thought … ." Crystal stopped talking, seeing her job in a new way and making a snap decision. "Okay. I'll do better. You'll see."

"Good. And you're going to start doing better right now. I have to go see a man about an apartment. If Lucinda calls, I'll phone her back in an hour or so. I shouldn't be long."

"Right, boss. You've got it." Crystal and Julia changed places, so Crystal was by the register. Julia wound her way into the back office and grabbed her coat. She checked her appearance in the mirror briefly, and headed towards the front door.

"And no closing so you can meet your new girlfriend," she underlined, as she pulled the door open and left.

∞

It was close to noon by the time Lucinda and Jasmine extricated themselves from the end of the Marketing meeting. Lucinda all but skipped from the room, buoyed by a major win, followed by an awed Jasmine and a shell-shocked Stuartson. Jasmine started to speak, but Lucinda stopped her with a raised hand.

"Rule 1: never discuss battle tactics in enemy territory. Now, grab your coat and meet me by the elevator, we're going out to celebrate."

"But..."

Lucinda stopped and stared at Jasmine with an incredulous look. "What?"

"Well, what about Mr. Rivers? Now that our project is over, don't I go back to reporting to him?"

"Jasmine, since yesterday at 1:30, you have been working for me. I set that up in case you panned out. So far, I don't regret my decision. Bottom line: you won't be reporting to Rivers anymore. You'll be moving closer to my office, starting this afternoon. And you'll report only to me. No one else.

"And this project isn't over, by any means. It's just beginning! I've got the nod to proceed. Now I knock 'em dead with execution. It's time you saw how ideas become reality. I think you can help me, to be honest. Interested?"

Jasmine smiled widely, in awe of the performance she'd seen Lucinda give at the meeting and excited by Lucinda's underhanded praise. "Absolutely!" was all she said.

"So go get your coat and meet me by the elevator."

Jasmine nodded and rushed off. And Lucinda, a satisfied spring in her step, went off to her office to grab her own jacket and purse.

∞

Oliver couldn't concentrate, even on the retail shoe site he'd found himself perusing. He sighed, stretched slightly and shut down his computer. He knew he should be preparing for the meeting he had after his chiropractor's appointment this afternoon, but his heart wasn't in it. He pushed his chair out from his desk and stood, taking the jacket he'd placed over the back and gingerly slipping it on. He had to get out and work out the spasms forking across his kidneys. Anything but sit at this desk and obsess over a woman he didn't have the balls to pursue, despite her open invitation. He could head to his appointment after he was finished walking or doing whatever he was doing. He just had to get out.

Susan stood when she saw Oliver exit his office with his jacket on and briefcase in hand.

"What about your..."

"Cancel it."

"And the..."

"Change it, cancel it. Do what you have to do. I'm out of the office until my four p.m.. I'll be back for that," he barked, and immediately felt regretful. Susan hardly deserved the tone he couldn't help. He knew who he was angry with, and it wasn't Susan.

"Fine," she said and sat, not without letting her boss know she felt ill-treated. "I'll see you at four. Sir."

∞

Lucinda and Jasmine stood outside the Manolo Blahnik office building waiting for a cab. Lucinda was talking animatedly into her cell phone.

"Yes, Julia. It went wonderfully. Our 'For Every Woman' campaign will be going ahead full steam starting immediately." She paused, listening carefully but still trying to wave down a vacant cab.

"Yes. We'll have to meet to go over the specifics. Yes. No, this afternoon I can't do. I have an appointment. But tomorrow would work. All right. Can you make it for ten a.m.?"

A cab came to a screeching halt in front of them and Lucinda and Jasmine scurried inside.

"The Appalachian." Lucinda said to the driver, then resumed her conversation with Julia.

"Perfect. Yes. They loved Sophia. We'll speak of all that tomorrow. All right." Lucinda flipped her phone shut, and paused over what had to be included on the agenda for her meeting with Julia. Then she turned to Jasmine, rewarding her with a rare smile.

"It's all coming together, Jasmine. Enjoy the ride!"

TWENTY-TWO

OLIVER HAD found himself shuffling about for hours. He hadn't stopped for lunch as he'd planned. He hadn't done much of anything except let his mind wander. And by the time he flagged down a cab to take him to his chiropractor's appointment, he was feeling somewhat himself again.

Oliver hated doctor's offices. The muted silence that consumed waiting rooms oppressed him. They made him nervous and jittery. But the pain in his lower back had not gone away, so he had no choice but to go or he'd be popping pain medication like they were Smarties. He sighed and pushed open the door to Dr Warshinsk's office and checked in with the receptionist.

"He's running a little behind, Mr. Garcia. Have a seat, and I'll let you know when he can see you."

Oliver sat less than happily, and picked up an obscenely out-of-date magazine. He started to flip casually through it, not caring what he saw. He just wanted to have his back feel better, have his life feel better.

∞

Lucinda got out of the cab in font of Dr Warshinsk's building and sent Jasmine back to Manolo with instructions to move her personal belongings to a cubicle closer to Lucinda's office. Lucinda headed inside with the Manolo Blahnik bag tucked under her arm – the bribe shoes neatly wrapped inside. The tension she'd been feeling between her shoulder blades

seemed to have abated a great deal since her departure from
the Marketing meeting this morning, but because of the trouble
she'd gone through to get this appointment, she felt obliged to
go and get adjusted. She had a bit of time to play with now;
the pressure was off until the next big push. She might as well
nip any brewing issues with her spine before they occurred.

She walked into Dr Warshinsk's waiting room and smiled
sweetly at the receptionist, swinging the Manolo bag in front
of her as she walked up to the counter.

"You must be Lucinda." The woman beamed at her, all but
snatching the bag from Lucinda's hand.

"I must indeed!" Lucinda replied rather flippantly, adding
"and you're ... Laura ... right?"

"Yes. I'll just tuck these in the back. I'll be right with you."
Lucinda smiled sweetly until the receptionist's back was
turned, then let out a sigh. Ugh. Who could bear to be nice all
the time? It took way too much energy.

"Dr Warshinsk is running a bit behind, Lucinda. Why don't
you have a seat? I know he'll be able to squeeze you in very
soon."

Lucinda nodded, dismissing Laura and heading for a chair.
As she turned and saw who the only other patient in the waiting
room was, she almost gasped aloud. The Letch. Fantasy Man.
The 'stooping shoe' creature! Son of a bitch, she thought,
what's he doing here? Then she thought about his hunched
position in the elevator, and accepted the coincidence.

He didn't look up as she took a seat across from him, thank
goodness. He had his nose firmly planted in a *Time* magazine.

Lucinda counted this as a small blessing. She took a notebook out of her briefcase and started making notes of issues to discuss with Julia the following morning.

Oliver had looked up sharply when the door to Dr Warshinsk's office swung open. He almost groaned out loud when he saw the goddess from the elevator saunter in. Had her heels not been muffled by the short pile carpeting, he certainly would have. Of all his rotten luck, he thought, the person he wanted to see most, and was dreading seeing most in the world, was about to share a waiting room with him. He buried his face in whatever magazine he was holding.

He watched in awe as she swung the bag across the desk towards the receptionist. It was a Manolo Blahnik bag! How could he not recognize it! He felt his heart skip a beat and he started salivating. Of course. Of course that's why he adored her shoes so much.

It was all making sense now. She must work at Manolo Blahnik! Now doubly embarrassed, he buried his face in his magazine, hoping she wouldn't notice him as she sat down.

He was drawn once again to her shoes. He pulled the magazine down a bit so he could discreetly peek over the top. Yes, those were leather. They looked as soft as a baby's bum, he thought to himself, and physically twitched with a need to touch them. He saw her look up sharply and he redirected his gaze back to some insufferable article in the magazine.

That bastard is scoping out my shoes again, Lucinda thought, and smiled a bit to herself. He's got it bad and doesn't quite know what to do. Good God! His hands are trembling! I should go and put him out of his misery she thought wickedly, and slid the pad of paper back into her briefcase.

Oh shit, Oliver thought! She's recognized me! He cursed his desire for shoes, wanted to curse this bloody woman. He felt horribly exposed, frighteningly vulnerable.

With the ache in his back worsening as he sat frozen on the uncomfortable chairs in the waiting room, he couldn't flee the doctors' office without having to wait days for another appointment. He glanced at his watch. It was 2:15 p.m. Please let them call me in now. *Now!* Please oh please, he begged to himself. Out of his peripheral vision he saw Legs standing and walking in his direction. He tried to refocus on the article, but was interrupted by a low voice next to him.

"Hello again."

Oliver looked up sharply into Lucinda's eyes. He's frightened to death, Lucinda thought.

"I *did* see you in the elevator this morning, didn't I?"

Oliver swallowed deeply and, barely trusting his voice, he muttered "Ah, yes. That was me."

"I couldn't help noticing that you were admiring my shoes." She crossed her glorious legs, attracting Oliver's gaze.

"You like these ones, do you?"

"The shoes are glorious. I like the legs they're attached to as well." Oh Jesus, Oliver thought, did I just say that out loud?

"Hmm." Lucinda said, playing with him a bit by rotating her ankle around and around. "I'm partial to these as well," she said, squaring down his gaze. "Is it the fact they're Manolo Blahniks that's got you excited?" Her smile was 'acid light'.

Lucinda and Oliver both looked up as the receptionist called her name.

"Well, ah…" He had never felt so tongue-tied.

"I'll see you around the building, no doubt." It was anything but an invitation.

"I hope so," he replied lamely, burning with humiliation. He buried his head back into the magazine as the echo of her heels on the linoleum carried down the hallway.

In his mind's memory, his gaze once again moved upward, over delicate ankles and curved calves. They followed upward to find Jasprinder's face beaming down at him. Jesus wept, he was a sorry idiot of a man. But she wanted him anyway, warts and all.

Giving his head a shake, he grabbed his cell phone from the inside pocket of his suit jacket and hit redial. He couldn't help but smile as a voice answered on the other end of the line.

"Jasprinder Singh?" he asked, more tentatively than ever before, "Would you join me for dinner tonight? I want and need your company." He could almost feel her smile carry through his handset, and he smiled in return.

EPILOGUE

THERE IS nothing more invigorating than being backstage at a New York Fashion Week show at Bryant Park. The place positively hums with activity. Divas screech, while hair and make-up stylists attempt to calm. Production Assistants yell into walkie-talkies, wildly waving them over their heads in a vain attempt to improve reception with front-of-house staff. Organizers bustle, attempting to herd the cats into their appropriate places.

Clipboard clutched under her arm, Lucinda observed it all, occasionally barking out orders that would make even the most seasoned NYFW veteran stop short. She navigated her way calmly and swiftly through the bustle, clearly on a mission. People instinctively cleared a path.

Jasmine thought her head was going to explode off her shoulders. Never in a thousand years did she ever expect to be standing where she was. The positive cacophony of yells and sea of technicians, models and workers surrounding her was overwhelming. It was worse than Times Square at rush-hour during Christmas. She shuddered in memory, but was hooked on the energy. Insane it might be, but she knew many of the players now, and delighted in what was about to happen.

She took a few steps up an open iron staircase leading to the lighting grid above, out of the fray, hoping to catch her breath for a moment and look around.

From that vantage point, Jasmine surveyed the organized chaos. She saw Julia futzing about with the shoulder straps on her gown, looking like she was in the middle of an argument with a couple of dressers. One of them was attempting to slip her feet into a pair of feathered mules while the other was struggling to zip up the back of her form-fitting gown. Sophia deftly stepped in, shooing the dressers away and placing two hands on Julia's shoulders. Jasmine couldn't hear what transpired between the two of course, but she could see Julia's shoulders visibly relax. Sophia turned her, deftly pulled the zipper up Julia's back, handed her the shoes and directed her towards the hair stations before slipping in between the racks and out of sight.

She could also see Vonda standing at the staging area, headset precariously resting on the straight-haired wig she was wearing. Vonda could be a meddling pain-in-the-butt, Jasmine had come to learn, but she had certainly been a lifesaver tonight. With the massively tall heels she was wearing and her own extraordinary height, she stood a full head above everyone and could keep track of even the flakiest queen just by sight. More practically, just when things seemed to get completely out of control, she would boom out orders or directions or call for specific models, her strong voice carrying over the din.

Right now, Vonda's voice was lashing two dressers into shape. The effect brought a smile to Jasmine's face, quickly suppressed as she realized who else would have heard Vonda. She scanned the scene in front of her, looking for signs of her boss.

Jasmine couldn't actually see Lucinda, but could see the path she cut through the crowds as she bee-lined towards the racks where a flustered-looking Julia had been standing moments before. As Vonda's voice reached Lucinda, she stopped in her track, spun on her heel and beat a furious path back towards the staging area. Who the hell was yelling orders? She gave the orders, damn it! She yelled them out over the normal behind-the-scenes chaos – no one else. If everyone else needed to communicate, well that's what they made those asinine walkie-talkies for. But nobody better forget that this was Lucinda's show. Her work. Her baby!

Jasmine cursed under her breath. She still hadn't lost her awe of Lucinda, but had learned that part of her job was to get between her boss and any unfortunate target. Lucinda's rages were terrible to behold, but if you weren't the object of her anger the clashes could offer moments of inner hilarity. She left the little sanctuary she'd found and headed towards the staging area herself. This one could get ugly, maybe. This one, she wanted to see.

By the time Lucinda had plowed her way to the big black monstrosity she found at the head of the runway, she was fired up, her nerves getting the better of her.

"We're on schedule?" she asked, foregoing a greeting.

"Yes, ma'am. Completely." Vonda didn't even bother to raise her eyes from the clipboard full of notes she held. This wasn't the first time the two had clashed.

"I heard Siobhan was late. You know how important it is that this show…"

Vonda cut Lucinda off. "She was 20 minutes late but we got her caught up. She should be finishing in makeup right now, but I'll have to check."

"You shouldn't have to check. If you were doing your job correctly, you would know." Lucinda's stance changed, her edginess taking on an antagonistic flare, coiling for a fight.

Vonda, responding to the aggression, took half a step forward, towering over Lucinda. "What I know, Miss Lucinda, is how to run this ship."

"Vonda, what I see is a dressing area in shambles, PAs scurrying around putting out your fires and saving your ass."

Tense moments passed as Vonda stood, fish-mouthed, astounded that Lucinda would call her out so publicly over something so blatantly incorrect. It was Vonda's breaking point.

"Not on my watch. No you didn't."

"Yep, I guess I did."

Vonda, incensed, dropped her clipboard to the ground and started taking off her shoes to start a real catfight. The mini-woman was going down!

Jasmine showed up just in time to hold Lucinda back.

"I should fire you right now." Lucinda hissed at Vonda.

"You could, but then you'd be in for a pile of chaos."

"What makes you think you're so capable?" If it was possible for someone of Lucinda's size to look down on someone as big as Vonda, those words did it. Vonda gave Lucinda an incredulous once-over, snapped her bare heels together and saluted.

"Captain Marcus Tomlinson, United States Marine Corps, Retired." For the first time in recent memory, Lucinda was speechless.

"Don't ask, don't tell, Miss Lucinda." Vonda added much more quietly. She paused, wondering if Lucinda would rip her a new one. When that didn't happen, she dipped down to slip back on her stilettos and retrieve her clip board.

"Right then." Vonda said, her bow hiding a satisfied smile, and giving Lucinda a moment to recover. Rising, she cupped a hand around one ear, listening. "Copy that," she said – deliberately demurely – into her walkie.

"It's time," she whispered to herself, then boomed over all the background cacophony, "Final line up, Ladies! Now or never!" PAs were heard echoing Vonda all over the dressing area. Vonda had made her point.

"Can I do my job now?" Vonda asked acerbically, looking down on Lucinda.

"Sure. You can most certainly do the job I'm paying you to do." Lucinda spun and walked away without acknowledging what she'd heard, her eyes staying focused on the shoes that had started lining up down the runway. Jasmine and Vonda's eyes met, rolled at each other, then with only a faint grin, Jasmine scurried after Lucinda, knowing without thought she would never mention what she'd just witnessed.

Vonda did one final head count, checking styling and the order of the models as the house lights dimmed. Lucinda and Jasmine both made their way to the monitors located behind the staging area scrims.

Make it or break it time, thought Jasmine, hoping for the best.

Make it time, thought Lucinda, ever confident.

∞

The hum of the audience died down with the dimming of the house lights – the only illumination remaining was the white fluorescent glow of the Manolo Blahnik logo on the backdrop located at the head of the runway.

As the music amped up and the models' excitement flared, so did Lucinda's anxiety. This was it. In about 15 minutes she'd either be lauded or be out of a job. She held her breath as the monitors showed the first model's entrance onto the runway. Thomasina stopped at the start of the runway as she was supposed to, backlit only by the Manolo sign. Five, four, three, two, Lucinda counted down. And then, right on cue, the spotlights turned on, highlighting Thomasina's feet wearing a spectacular pair of blue sequined slingbacks. As she strutted down towards the end of the runway, gridded spotlights turned on in succession following the shoes while keeping the model herself in the dark.

When the queen hit the end of the runway, three powerful lights lit her up at once as she struck a triumphant and outrageous pose. The audience gasped at the revelation of the true identity of the first model. It was only when the gasps and shocked murmurs were replaced with thunderous applause did Lucinda breathe easier. It was going to be a success! She refused to allow a triumphant smile to show.

With each model strutting and posing, the audience applause continued in a constant roar, and when Julia, the final model, was finally revealed by the spotlights at the end of the runway, not only was there applause and some hoots (as there were for Sophia's walk) but from the back of the seating area came a rousing chant of 'Julia! Julia!'.

Jasmine and Lucinda smiled at each other. They'd pulled it off.

Vonda's booming "Line up for the finale, ladies!" reached them, pulling Lucinda and Jasmine's attention back to the monitors. Queens were herded into their final order by sweating PAs. Lights were re-cued. Music was synched. If the finale worked, Lucinda knew – unconsciously recognizing Vonda's importance to the presentation – the campaign should work. She refused to consider Vonda's confession.

Despite her exhilaration as the finale began, Lucinda couldn't believe who had caught her eye out in the audience. She waited until the overhead spot light did another sweep along the side of the runway, stopping and swinging past celebrities and fashionistas alike.

Son of a bitch. It was her elevator fetishist, sitting with his… beautiful Indian girlfriend? The pair had been smiling at each other when Oliver had leaned in to whisper into her ear. She'd laughed at whatever he had said, then the spotlight had moved on, plunging the couple back into darkness. Well well well, Lucinda thought. Perhaps she'd made a mistake about the elevator man. Hell, perhaps the show had garnered at least two new clients.

Lucinda's back stiffened slightly as the finale catwalk run started. Again the models were in the dark with only their shoes illuminated by the spotlights. On their return strut towards the base of the catwalk, each model took a spot along the runway, all looking out towards the audience. It was only then that lyrics were included into the thumping base line that had been playing throughout the show. A mix of Whitney Houston's classic "I'm Every Woman" brought the crowd to their feet. When the spotlights started flashing alternately between the shoes and the models' faces, the crowd went wild. The queens all started their own lip-sync routines to the music. The audience ate it up. And as the last refrains of the music played, queens dramatically finished up and strutted proudly offstage.

As the last model cleared the runway into the backstage area, Lucinda and Jasmine beamed at each other. It had worked perfectly, a concept perfectly executed. Jasmine's arms moved from where they'd been clutched round her middle, making motions as if to hug Lucinda. Lucinda's eyebrows quirked up, shutting Jasmine down with a pointed stare. Instead she took Jasmine's hand in her own and shook it vigorously.

"I knew the idea would work! And you did well, Jasmine. Thank you for all your help."

Jasmine blushed under the praise, despite knowing it was deserved. "Well, thank you for letting me work for you on this project. This has been an amazing experience on many levels."

"I'm sure it has been." Lucinda smiled softly, thinking she might just have a word with Personnel about hiring the young intern. Then, all business once again, "Stay until you've got all the shoes packed and the courier has picked them up to take them back to Manolo. Then you're free to go. I'll see you at 8:45 Monday morning. My office. We'll deconstruct the night and see what can be improved upon for next time. In the meantime, I've got some press to take care of."

"Of course, Lucinda. There's a place out front that's been set up for the press call." Both were more than happy to get back to a working relationship.

Jasmine scurried back towards the dress racks where Sophia had cracked open a couple of champagne bottles. Lucinda made a quick motion to Julia, and together they pulled apart two side curtains and stepped out into the front of the house to meet the press, the smile on their faces sincere and genuine. Lucinda still had that smile on her face as she descended the short staircase to the audience floor and did a quick scan of the emptying seating area. Julia went ahead to where the press had been wrangled into one corner, cameras and microphones poised and ready.

Lucinda took a moment to take a deep breath and enjoy the triumphant moment. A few people still milled about – some just spectators and others bloggers making updates on laptops precariously balanced on knees. She caught the eye of her neighbour where he was sitting in deep conversation with his lady. There's got to be an interesting story there, she thought to herself. I wonder how they met?

Lucinda didn't approach him, nor did he break off his conversation. She did give him a smile and a knowing wink. She made a mental note to discretely ask him what size shoe he wore when they next bumped into each other. She could then do a little James Bond and have a plainly wrapped pair of pumps delivered to his door. She smiled again to herself, and stepped confidently towards the throngs of reporters.

∞

Jasmine was having a ball. Vonda had literally pulled her out from between the racks to join the party. Now, surrounded by giddy queens, she was being given more style and hair advice than she knew what to do with. She drew the line at a post-show makeover, but had plenty of invites to the Wolves Den for some hands-on experience. Her friends back home would be shocked. Jasmine couldn't wait.

A familiar, unassuming man caught her eye as she polished off her second flute of champagne. She excused herself from the ladies and approached him.

"I'm surprised and glad to see you here! Did you see any of the show?"

"If Boss-lady asks, no. But between you and me, it was great," Hank said, somewhat sheepishly.

"Would you like me to find her for you?" Jasmine asked, gesturing towards the bouquet of flowers in Hank's hands. "She's doing press stuff in the front of the house."

"No. Not necessary. In fact, she'll probably be pissed that I crossed the threshold and that we talked," adding as he thrust the flowers towards Jasmine, "but would you mind just making sure she gets these? I'll wait outside."

"Sure, Hank. Happy to." Jasmine tucked the flowers into the crook of her elbow as Hank turned to go. He quickly turned back.

"Jasmine? Thank you. For everything."

"Truly my pleasure," she said with a smile "I'll get these right to her."

∞

When Jasmine finally found Lucinda and Julia, the interviews were just wrapping up. "… yes, of course diversity is incredibly important in today's society. That's why a percentage of each pair of shoes sold under this campaign will be donated to the Trevor Project." Lucinda looked over at Jasmine and quirked an eyebrow at the flowers she held.

"Will you all excuse me? Julia will be happy to answer any further questions." Lucinda backed away, letting Julia have the spotlight to herself, and pulled Jasmine aside.

"Sorry to interrupt, Lucinda, but these were delivered for you backstage." Jasmine thrust the flowers into Lucinda's arms. Lucinda plucked the card from where it had been nestled in the blooms and read it. The flush that crept up her neck and settled in her cheeks didn't go unnoticed by Jasmine. She smiled up at her boss.

"I'm, ah, just going to head backstage again.… . Have a great weekend."

"Oh yes," Lucinda breathed, her eyes not leaving the card. "You too. See you Monday."

Jasmine and Lucinda parted ways, but Jasmine took one more look over the front of house. She saw Julia in her element, soaking up the attention from the photographers and fielding questions like a pro. She saw PAs doing quick trash sweeps through the rows of chairs flanking the runway, and saw Lucinda slipping out the front doors. That made her smile too. She slipped through the curtains and into the darkness of backstage.

Jasmine was finishing up logging the shoeboxes for the courier to pick up when a delicate voice cut into her concentration.

"Jasmine?" She looked up and saw Julia, now out of her gown and in a long skirt and sweater set, holding her pair of mules by their heels.

"Hey, Julia. Great show. Congratulations! You must be really proud."

"I'm happy, sure. Hopefully this will lead to some big things."

"If Lucinda has anything to do with it at all, it will." They both laughed.

"Are you heading to the after-party at the Wolves Den? It's going to be quite the party."

"No, but I wish I could. I've got things to finish up here, and then I've got a date with my bed. You?"

Julia chuckled, "Yes, I'm going. With a date."

"Really?" Jasmine tried not to sound too surprised. "Anyone I've met connected with the show?"

"Nope. Completely out of the lifestyle. But he's fabulous."

"Next time we meet up, you'll have to tell me everything."

"I'll do that for sure." She handed over the shoes and Jasmine deftly slipped them into tissue paper and into their appropriate box. Both fell silent for a moment, a moment of awkwardness as they realized that, however different their worlds were, they sensed a basis for a friendship.

"Well," Julia started, "I'd better get going and not keep the man waiting."

"Have a good weekend, Julia. We'll talk with you soon."

"Good night." Julia swept in and placed a brief kiss on either of Jasmine's cheeks, then stepped away, throwing a little wave over her shoulder as she walked away.

It was eerily quiet backstage now that all the employees and models had left for the after-party. Jasmine made quick work of the itemized shoe list. Then, as she waited for the courier to arrive, she sat for a moment and took a deep breath.

It had been quite a whirlwind couple of months since that first fateful meeting at Rovers. She'd learned a lot – some of it the hard way – but was completely happy. Lucinda seemed happy with her work as well, and that meant a lot. Jasmine finally felt like she belonged. She'd found a job she was good at and she'd made some friends along the way. She was living the dream. Her dream.

Made in the USA
Charleston, SC
05 September 2013